"I am the [...] here to me[...] and gazed at Claybourne Honeycutt.

Good looks could certainly mask a scoundrel, and she suspected that's exactly what he was.

His lowering those long dark lashes over his eyes for a moment infuriated her. She pointed to the white dress on the dress form. "I have been making this for Breanna's marriage to you. Now, you can tell me what you know about this, or I can contact the authorities."

His focus seemed to be on the wedding dress, and he appeared thoughtful for a moment. Then his deep blue gaze fell upon her again. "What about this scenario?" His head lowered just a bit, and his eyes seemed to dance. "Maybe you don't have a sister. Maybe you made this up, having seen my name on papers passing through the office on the mainland."

Her jaw developed a mind of its own, and she didn't seem able to close her mouth. His audacity rendered her speechless.

"Maybe you have been influenced by this picture-bride activity and decided to become one yourself." He gestured toward the wedding dress. "You say you were reluctant for your sister to come to Hawaii. But you're making a wedding dress for her?" He scoffed. "Your stories don't add up. Hold it. Don't move."

Moving had not been an option since he walked through the door. But that sounded like a threat, and she was now about to bolt. Just then, the spark that had been in his photo appeared in his eyes. What was it? Daring? Skepticism? Challenge? He grinned. "I can picture you in that dress. Looks like it's just your size. I propose that the dress is yours, and it is you, not some"—he spread his hands for emphasis—"some illusive sister, who wishes to marry."

"Why. . .why would I want to marry you?" she managed to say above the thundering of her heart.

YVONNE LEHMAN is an award-winning, bestselling author of mainstream, mystery, romance, young adult, and women's fiction. Founder and director of her own writers conference, she now directs the Blue Ridge Mountains Christian Writers Conference held annually at the Ridgecrest/LifeWay Conference Center near Asheville, North Carolina.

HEARTSONG PRESENTS

Picture
Bride

Yvonne Lehman

Heartsong Presents

To Carmen Leal for her suggestion of a picture-bride story, and to DiAnn Mills for her invaluable comments.

Author's Note:

The term *picture bride* refers to the practice in the early twentieth century in which tens of thousands of immigrant workers (chiefly Japanese and Korean) in Hawaii and on the West Coast of the United States selected brides—sight unseen—from their native countries. A matchmaker (also called a *marriage handler* or *go-between*) paired bride and groom using only photographs and family recommendations of the possible candidates. This is a practice akin to traditional arranged marriages, the securing of brides from Europe by the early settlers of the American continent, and the concept of mail-order brides.

A note from the Author:

I love to hear from my readers! You may correspond with me by writing:

> **Yvonne Lehman**
> **Author Relations**
> **PO Box 721**
> **Uhrichsville, OH 44683**

ISBN 978-1-60260-567-1

PICTURE BRIDE

All scripture quotations are taken from the King James Version of the Bible.

All of the characters and events in this book are fictitious. Any resemblance to actual persons, living or dead, or to actual events is purely coincidental.

Our mission is to publish and distribute inspirational products offering exceptional value and biblical encouragement to the masses.

PRINTED IN THE U.S.A.

one

Spring 1910, San Francisco

"This is so unfair."

Mary Ellen Colson smiled at her sister's outburst. She looked up from the papers on her desk and at Breanna, who mumbled, "Europe." After filing the papers in the metal cabinet, Breanna picked up another folder. "Japan."

She walked to another cabinet, and a ray of late afternoon sun shone against the tendrils of her golden blond hair falling gracefully along the sides of her pretty face.

Having filed that stack, Breanna came over for others. Her eyes, usually as blue as a peaceful sky, seemed filled with emotion reminiscent of a cloudy day.

"What now?" Mary Ellen said, although she'd heard every reason for her sister's dissatisfaction. Breanna called it boredom. Mary Ellen called it teenage wanderlust.

Breanna sighed. "I spend my days in school, afternoons in this stuffy old office, and nights in the dingy boardinghouse, studying. I mean, that's my life. And old Mr. Crank won't give me a penny of my own money." Making circles with her thumbs and index fingers, she put them up to her eyes.

"That's not funny," Mary Ellen chided.

Breanna struck a pert pose. "Then why did you laugh?"

"Because of the face you made. Not because you called Mr. Frank a crank."

"That's how he looks with his mouth turned down and his eyes squinted behind those dark-rimmed glasses."

Mary Ellen picked up the letter opener and sliced the edge of another envelope. "What would you do if Mr. Frank gave you money?"

Without hesitation, Breanna picked up the sides of her dress, exposing her ankles above the flats she wore to school. She curtsied to a make-believe partner and danced a graceful imitation of a reel. "I'd see the world."

After a few more dainty steps, her expression turned serious. She grasped the sides of the desk. "Oh, Mary Ellen. People pass through this office, mainly only in letters and folders. But they represent people traveling to and from all parts of the world. Outside these windows are the real people coming and going. I want to be one of those persons who does something. Who goes somewhere."

"You're still in school, Breanna."

"I'll graduate in a couple of months. But I won't have any money until I'm twenty."

"That's only a little over two years."

"But I don't want to get stuck. Like you. You've never been anywhere. You don't meet any. . .men." She groaned. "I mean, I know you're more like Uncle Harv. But I'm not." She stomped a foot and nodded. "I'm different."

"You're going to be penniless if you don't finish that filing."

With a moan and slump of her shoulders, Breanna picked up the stack, laid it on Uncle Harv's desk, and resumed her filing.

Mary Ellen took the folded paper from the envelope she held, but her thoughts delved into the past when the 1906 earthquake and fire had taken their parents. Any fanciful dreams of hers had been swallowed up by the quake and burned up in the fire. Being five years older than Breanna, she'd tried be like a mother to her. So many times, she felt she'd failed.

And being like Uncle Harv? Mary Ellen knew Breanna was referring to his being a confirmed bachelor. That's how he liked his life. Mary Ellen didn't like the idea of being a spinster. But she had never allowed herself to consider taking a man seriously as long as Breanna needed her. And she did need her, whether or not she knew it.

Mary Ellen understood the job was boring to Breanna—

although she worked it only a couple of hours after school.

Much of the office work was routine, checking arrival and departure passenger lists. Accuracy of names, surnames, age, gender, ethnicity, nationality of the last country of permanent residence, and arrival date or departure dates needed to be noted. If the individual was going to join with a friend or relative, that had to be checked out.

With a sigh, Mary Ellen unfolded the form in her hands, expecting it to be like thousands she'd dealt with over the past few years.

But her fingers brushed against a square of photo-quality paper as it fell to the desk. She read the writing on the back:

> *American citizen, seeking a young American*
> *blond woman for a bride.*
> *Occupation: sugar plantation in Hawaii*
> *I am a moral person.*
> *If you can help, please reply to:*
> *C. Honeycutt*
> *General Delivery, Post Office*
> *Hilo, Hawaii*

This was highly unusual. Mary Ellen turned the photo over and gazed at something even more unusual. Staring at her was a man with a perfect face. One couldn't be sure of color in a black-and-white photo, but the wavy hair and eyes were definitely dark. Instead of a posed expression, he had a rather roguish look with a slight tilt of his head, a hint of a grin on his lips. His eyes seemed to tease.

She estimated his age anywhere from twenty-five to thirty. Hearing her breath, caused by an increase in heart rate, she placed her hand on her chest and felt the fast beating.

That was unusual, too, her having a reaction over a photo of an appealing man as if she were a teenager like Breanna seeing an acclaimed stage actor. Oh, but Breanna could have a conniption just seeing a boy on the street.

Well, she could look at the form. This man could be seeking an American he'd lost touch with.

No. The information on the form was from a Japanese male, aged forty-two.

The photo should not have been with the Japanese man's form. Maybe she should contact C. Honeycutt and inform him the office did not handle requests like this.

The return address revealed it came from the immigration office. But Mr. C. wanted a reply to general delivery at a post office. This was by no means official.

Maybe. . . she shouldn't bother Uncle Harv with it. Perhaps the man got caught up in the thousands of picture brides arriving in Hawaii and impulsively did this to see what might happen. What kind of man would do such a thing?

Well, a man looking for an American wife? But why blond?

Despite what Breanna thought, Mary Ellen was not completely devoid of appreciating a little joke. And this did give her a moment's respite from the usual business of the day. This Mr. C.'s occupation was working at a sugarcane plantation.

Uncle Harv, who had been to Hawaii to inspect their office, had spoken of green sugarcane fields flowing across the land like waves across the ocean.

"What are you doing, Mary Ellen?"

"Huh?"

Mary Ellen left the green cane fields and focused on Breanna, sitting in Uncle Harv's chair. "You've been staring at your desk forever, and you're about to twist the button off your blouse."

"Oh." Mary Ellen stopped twisting. "I was daydreaming."

Breanna giggled. "I didn't think you did that."

Neither did I. She eased the form over the photo. Breanna noticed and came over. "What do you have there?"

"Just the usual form and—"

Before Mary Ellen could stop her, Breanna picked up the photo. "Oh, he's gorgeous. If I had a button on my blouse, I'd twist it off, too." She sighed. "Now see, if I could travel—"

Her words stopped in midair when she turned the photo over and read the message. Then she looked at the form. "These came in the same envelope?"

"They did. But this photo should not be in here."

Breanna gasped like she'd received an early Christmas present. "Oh, I think it should."

"No." Mary Ellen reached for the photo. "We have to show this to Uncle Harv."

"My foot!" Breanna held it away. "I have to think about this."

You?

Mary Ellen should answer that, for once in her life, maybe she would like to think about something different, however illusive. But that was foolish, and she couldn't blame it on teenage immaturity. She was twenty-three years old and had made a commitment to be there for Breanna as long as her sister needed her.

Breanna returned to Uncle Harv's desk and moistened her red, heart-shaped smiling lips with her tongue, as if the man in the photo were good enough to eat.

"Dream on if you want," Mary Ellen said. "Then come back to reality."

The door opened, and Uncle Harv walked in, looking his usual dapper, middle-aged self. "Good afternoon, ladies. How is everything?"

Mary Ellen opened her mouth to speak, but Breanna beat her to it. "Same as usual. Nothing out of the ordinary. Forms for your approval are right here." She laid her hands on the pile as if she had been the one who had reviewed them. "And I've filed folder after folder all afternoon."

"Good." He smiled at her, nodded at Mary Ellen, stuck his cane in the ceramic urn by the door, and hung his top hat on a coatrack peg.

Mary Ellen shot a warning glance at Breanna, who simply stood and motioned for her uncle to sit at his desk. He sat, straightened his tie, and focused on the forms he needed to review, then approve or disapprove.

Breanna continued filing and slid a glance at Mary Ellen. Her face was the epitome of innocence. There was no photo in sight, but she did have a large skirt pocket.

Mary Ellen knew what she would say if she were as young as Breanna, or as pretty, or as impulsive, or as lacking in sense.

Even if the photo and message were a mistake or a prank, she would have said something like, *I saw him first. . . .*

This is so unfair.

&

Green fields of long, slender sugarcane leaves rippled in the wind like ocean waves. The breeze tugged at her hair, her dress, and her heart. An emotional breathless feeling was overwhelming as a tall, dark-haired man with eyes full of mischief strode toward her. His smile meant she was the joy of his life and she—

She began to cough and struggled to sit up, trying to get her breath.

"Mary Ellen, are you all right?"

After several deep breaths and attempts at clearing her throat, Mary Ellen managed to speak. "I got. . .choked."

"Ugh! Maybe you swallowed a bug."

It was Mary Ellen's turn to say, "Ugh." She pictured a roach like the occasional ones showing up in the kitchen, causing the cook and landlady to go on a cleaning frenzy and sprinkle powdered poison in pantries and corners. Swallowing a bug wasn't what happened. "It was my own saliva."

Breanna laughed, getting up to pull the string for the overhead light bulb, dispelling the faint morning sunrays seeping through the curtains. "Let that be a lesson. Don't spit in your sleep."

"I'll remember." Mary Ellen slipped to the side of the bed and stepped into her slippers. What she intended to remember was to dispense with foolish dreams. She had not gone to sleep thinking about Mr. C., except she'd prayed Breanna would forget the photo and any notion of going to Hawaii to meet a stranger.

"Did you—" No, she wouldn't ask if Breanna had dreamed. "Did you sleep well?"

"Like a newborn baby." A playful look settled in her eyes. "Until somebody started choking herself."

Maybe Breanna hadn't taken the photo episode seriously. Neither of them mentioned it or going anywhere except school and work while they dressed for the day. Soon they descended the stairs to go into the dining room for breakfast.

After Mary Ellen took the cable car to the office, she poured hot tea into a cup. "Uncle Harv." She set the cup and saucer in front of him. "On your trip to Hawaii, did you see the Honeycutt sugarcane plantation?"

"Of course, my dear. It's the largest on the big island. After the United States annexed the islands, I was sent there to ensure all those foreign workers and picture brides were needed."

"Did you meet any Honeycutts?"

After taking a sip of tea, he shook his head. "Don't believe I did. My contacts were government officials." He laughed lightly. "Although government officials are made up of businessmen and landowners. Why do you ask? Is there some discrepancy?"

His shoulders straightened, and he focused on her. Uncle Harv was meticulous about his work.

"I come across the name of Honeycutt quite often."

"Well, like I said, men and women are coming and going from those plantations all the time, and I'm sure you've seen the name on bags of sugar."

Honeycutt Sugar. Yes, she had. She'd never had occasion to buy any. She and Breanna ate most of their meals at Mrs. Bonemark's Boarding House and occasionally went to a restaurant.

"The Honeycutts are well respected, I'm sure."

He nodded. "The landowners are descendants of the early missionaries. Many are American, European, Scottish. Most of the workers are Asians, primarily from Japan."

Mary Ellen knew of the overpopulation of males in America and in Hawaii. Men had immigrated from Europe and Asia, looking for better jobs. The American citizens, however, could advertise for a mail-order bride through a catalog or correspond with Europeans and meet women through families, or photos, or in person. So why had Mr. C. sent that photo?

She'd been intrigued with the picture-bride process after coming to work for the immigration office. Some requests came to the U.S., but hundreds of Japanese women left their countries and voyaged to Hawaii each month to marry men they'd never met.

"Amazing, isn't it, Uncle? Men and women are willing to marry each other sight unseen."

He sniffed. "More amazing is that they marry at all."

At her gasp, he looked at her, and a rare spark touched his eyes. "I'm joking with you."

If he hadn't told her, she would not have known. Uncle Harv didn't joke.

He touched the bridge of his eyeglasses. "I'm not against marriage. It's just not for me."

She thought a hint of sadness touched his eyes, but they were immediately covered by his eyelids as he frowned at the papers in front of him. He picked up his cup, and if she hadn't known better, she'd have thought his hand shook a little. Was Uncle Harv getting old? But he was only in his mid-forties. Or did he have some kind of emotional tremor? She never thought of him as emotional.

A thought stabbed her. Breanna had described her as being like Uncle Harv. Did he pretend as much as she did? Pretend all was well and relationships didn't matter?

How did Breanna really see her? Was it not as a mother figure who put Breanna first, but as a domineering older sister who lacked human feelings? But she'd never wanted her sister feeling guilty that she'd sacrificed anything for her. She hadn't really. Breanna was her family. She loved her. They belonged together.

But now, Breanna wanted to break the bonds. That was part of growing up, she knew. Maybe, it was time for Mary Ellen to reveal she had some personality, had some impossible. . . dreams.

"Mary Ellen," she heard, and for an instant felt like she had when awakening from a dream, choking. "Are you all right?"

To be honest, no, she was not all right.

She was not content with her life being spent in this office. She was not content to try to keep Breanna from having fanciful dreams. She could not allow herself the luxury of dreaming.

Always. . .reality.

But suppose her imagination ran wild? Just for a moment?

"I was thinking, Uncle. You've traveled all over the world and say the United States is more prosperous than any other nation. Then why are so many also traveling to Hawaii?"

"Ah, my dear. Since America annexed Hawaii, it is not a foreign country. Hawaii is a paradise. A jewel in the sea. The new land of opportunity. It's like a conglomeration of all nations. On the island of Hawaii, you have the ocean and valleys at sea level; then you have the mountains, the tropical jungle, everything in one place—and a beauty unimaginable."

Mary Ellen caught her breath.

"There's always a soft breeze, and the sugarcane fields flow like gentle waves of an ocean as far as the eye can see." A trace of a smile touched his lips. "I've about had my fill of travel. But one place I wouldn't mind seeing again is Hawaii."

Could he possibly be a romantic at heart?

"Well," she said without putting a stop to her imagination now taking flight, "wouldn't the immigration office in Hawaii take you on as an inspector?"

"Surely. An American would be an asset to their office. Particularly one who has traveled the world. But I—" He shook his head. "I would not disrupt my life. It's planned. Settled."

"Would they hire an American woman who has worked in

an immigration office in America? Even if she speaks only English and a little classroom French?"

He had become cardboard again. Blank eyes looked at papers in front of him. Just as she turned to pull up the chair to her desk, he said, "With the proper recommendation, that is likely."

For the rest of the morning, before Uncle Harv had to go to the port of entry to oversee the work of immigration inspectors, Mary Ellen opened envelopes, put forms or letters into their appropriate folders or piles, and deposited the needed ones on his desk.

Their conversation appeared to be forgotten.

Perhaps Breanna had forgotten Mr. C.'s photo and had gone on to another dream. The man was too. . .too what?

Too mature for her sister—that's what.

In two months, Breanna would be eighteen, out of school, and moving on to college or finding a position if she didn't work with Uncle Harv. She could do as she wished.

That meant Mary Ellen could have the luxury of making her own dreams.

What would they be?

Perhaps she could take a job at the immigration office in Hawaii. Of course, she wouldn't leave her sister behind. And Mary Ellen had her inheritance, small but enough for her needs until she could get proper wages. She would check out that Mr. C. Maybe he would prefer a more mature blond woman than Breanna.

"You seem in particular good spirits today," her uncle said. "Different somehow."

She smiled and shrugged as if she didn't know what he meant. But after he left the office, she positioned her chin on her clasped hands and pictured fields of green waving gently in the breeze, and she dared to believe. . .in dreams.

Could it be that in Mary Ellen Colson's future there was paradise?

two

Hilo, Hawaii, one week earlier

Instead of taking the letters directly to the Hilo Post Office, he went in the opposite direction. He ducked into the Matti-Rose Inn.

Matilda caught him creeping down the hallway "What are you up to?" Her green eyes, set off by her thick red hair the color of Kilauea's volcanic fire on a dark night, must have guessed he was up to mischief.

"Emergency."

"The grandson of a missionary should be studying for the ministry, not sneaking around like he doesn't want anybody to see him."

"I just want to visit an inside bathroom. Maybe you shouldn't have installed those modern contraptions."

"Shouldn't you be working instead of being a *pupule kolohe.*"

He laughed at her calling him a *crazy rascal* in the Hawaiian language. Shaking his head, he put his arm against his waist, hoping the envelopes wouldn't slip down his pants leg.

"Oh, I smell my pie." She headed to the kitchen.

Getting no response when he tapped on the bathroom door, he entered, closed the door, and slid the lock.

He rescued the envelopes and sat on the commode beneath the water tank. The box labeled SCOTT PAPER COMPANY that would be filled with small squares of tissue made a good table. He ignored the stirring of uncertainty in his stomach. He'd planned this and would see it through.

There was nothing unusual about his being at the immigration office since much of his duties required that. But for a while, he'd made a habit of stopping by when Mr.

Hammeur was at lunch. Many times, it was his job to take the Japanese men to the office to help them fill out the forms for acquiring a wife. Too many men had lied about their age and the amount of money they had to lure some pretty little Japanese girl over here to marry them.

Well, now he understood better how a deceptive Japanese man might feel—guilty yet hopeful.

He'd offered to lick a few envelopes for Akemi when he saw the ones addressed to the office in San Francisco. He'd only pretended to moisten one of the flaps.

He slipped the photo into the envelope and licked the flap before he could change his mind. He left the bathroom and hurried out the front door before anyone could call to him and headed for the post office.

"We might be getting some special kind of mail from the mainland," he said to the clerk recently hired. Not that it mattered. Honeycutt mail was sent out and picked up at any time most days. "It will be addressed to C. Honeycutt for general delivery. Keep it separate from the other mail. I'll ask for it."

"No problem." The clerk took the letters. "All you have to do is ask for it."

Would it be that easy to get a beautiful blond from the American mainland?

Just ask?

ঌ

San Francisco

Mary Ellen kept glancing at the wall clock. Breanna always came straight to the office and rarely had after-school activities. At twenty minutes past the hour, her sister rushed in, breathless and with flushed cheeks.

"I was worried. Where've you been?"

"I stopped by the boardinghouse." She deposited her books onto Mary Ellen's desk and slipped out a photo that was tucked between the pages. "I had to find this."

She laid two photos in front of Mary Ellen. "Now, Miss Matchmaker. What do you think?"

Mary Ellen was not a matchmaker. She only matched up official forms and gave them to Uncle Harv, who approved or disapproved anyone requesting entry into the United States.

Mary Ellen would have to admit they appeared to be a perfect match—if Mr. C.'s request had been an official one.

The photo had been taken at Christmas when Breanna's light-colored hair hung in loose waves around her shoulders. She'd worn a stylish dress that Mary Ellen had made for Christmas. If Mr. C. saw that photo, he surely would be captivated by beautiful Breanna.

"Well, tell me." Breanna gripped the edge of the desk. "Is this the right picture to send?"

Mary Ellen needed to put aside her own foolish thoughts about Mr. C. The whole idea was preposterous. She looked up at her sister, who leaned over the desk. "If this were the right thing to do, this picture is the perfect one to send."

A delightful sound escaped Breanna's throat.

"This, however, is not the way to do things."

Breanna gazed at Mary Ellen. "We've talked about the hundreds and thousands who do this. Parents arrange marriages. Men order brides through catalogs. We work for an office that encourages the Asians to do that in Hawaii. So why is this so wrong?"

"It's wrong for you. It's just not right for us."

"Us?" Sadness settled in Breanna's eyes. "I'm a poor girl, without parents, without a dowry. What kind of man is going to be interested in the likes of me?"

"You're beautiful, Breanna. Everybody says that."

"A pretty face without money means nothing. I know I seem like a scatterbrain, but I don't want a man who would buy me because I'd look good on his arm."

Mary Ellen was glad to hear that.

"This is the best possibility I've had. Oh, the waiter at the restaurant, the half-dozen middle-aged friends of Uncle

Harv, the gawking fishermen, even the Asians who aren't supposed to look at me, the boys I go to school with, and the bachelor teachers. And yes, I've been introduced to some of the more acceptable men at church. They're not acceptable to me." Breanna lifted her chin saucily. "Nor to you, so I've been told."

Mary Ellen had said she didn't know a man who appealed to her enough to get serious about. There had been a connection with William Barr, an assistant in the boys' dorm when she'd worked at the orphanage as a seamstress. They'd taken long walks and had ridden over pastureland together. But when he became too serious, she'd reminded herself she'd taken the job to be near Breanna.

"Oh, please, Mary Ellen. Loan me the money for passage. All yours does anyway is sit in the bank drawing interest. This is like—" She placed one hand over another where her heart was likely pounding furiously with anticipation. "Like my big chance in life."

"You're impatient. In a couple of years, you'll have the money that's in your trust fund. You'll think this photograph is ridiculous."

"Really? Look again."

Mary Ellen dared not lower her gaze, but focused on the wall clock. She was not surprised when Breanna declared, "I'm going to Hawaii even if I have to swim."

Her sister had a stubborn streak that could be difficult to reason with. But she had to try. "Look, Breanna. Uncle Harv is your legal guardian. But I'm your sister and have tried to look after you."

Breanna had the consideration to nod and look down at her hands clasped in front of her skirt. "I know that, Mellie. You won't believe this, but I have listened to you. And I pray every night that I'll do what's right."

Mary Ellen had to squeeze away the moisture forming in her eyes. Her sister could get to her, especially by calling her by the name Breanna had used when just a toddler.

"Mellie, I can't be content here, and I'm not a child anymore."

But either she or Breanna had to be sensible, and which one was clear as day. "This is not the legal process."

"Oh pooh on legal process. This is personal. Now, what do I do? Do I just send my photo and wait to hear from Mr. C.?"

"If I'm the matchmaker, then let me handle it."

"Oh, you'll scare him away."

"This is a lifetime decision. What the Asians are doing is different. Their culture is different. They're accustomed to having a relative or matchmaker pair them up with someone. And it has worked for them. Sometimes I wonder if that's not better than. . .than. . .butterflies in the stomach and bells in the brain."

Breanna put her hands on her hips. "How would you know about that?"

Mary Ellen looked down at her desk, and her gaze fell on Mr. C.'s photo. Her heart could go pitter-patter as quickly as any other girl's. She sighed. "Hawaii is over twenty-six hundred miles away, and you don't know anyone there."

"But Uncle Harv does. He told us about those nice people from the tourism department and the two women he dearly loved, who ran an inn where he stayed. I even have a pamphlet here somewhere." She opened her notebook and pulled it out. "This was written by Mark Twain. You know him?"

"Who doesn't know the most popular columnist for the *Sacramento Union*!"

Breanna wasn't much for reading the daily news. At least she was reading that entertaining column by Twain.

" 'No alien land in all the world has any deep strong charm for me but that one,'" Breanna read. " 'No other land could so longingly and beseechingly haunt me, sleeping and waking. . . .'"

"Okay, Breanna. I'm the one who encouraged you to read his columns. And thousands of people are visiting there. I understand anyone could fall in love with that place. But. . ."

Mary Ellen closed her eyes rather than finish. Could she

honestly say she didn't see how anyone could fall in love with a photo? Of course she could say it. Instead, she shook her head.

"Mellie, will you help me write the letter?"

If she said no, Breanna would write it herself and not ask the appropriate questions. "Yes, I'll help you."

What would she write if Breanna had not snatched the photo from her and if she had been imprudent enough to contact Mr. C. for herself?

Mary Ellen picked up a blank sheet of paper and rolled it into the typewriter. "Study." She pointed to the schoolbooks.

"Yes, ma'am." Breanna hurried over to sit in Uncle Harv's chair and opened a book. She looked at Mary Ellen, who gave her a warning glance. Then she seemed to read her book in earnest.

Mary Ellen almost giggled as she readied her fingers to type.

She thought of writing *Dear Sweetheart*.

But of course she wouldn't type that.

She cleared her throat as if she had done such a silly thing. She could see his face in her mind, those dark teasing eyes. She could imagine he would laugh if she typed those words. The room, however, was soon filled with the *click-clack* of the typewriter keys striking the roller:

Dear Mr. C.:

Your photo with the contact information on the back arrived at the immigration office. Perhaps this was sent by mistake, or perhaps it is a practical joke from someone else since there was no official form attached.

If your intention is to find someone you've known, please inform us. If you are looking for an American bride at random, I would like to know that, too. If this is serious, please send more information.

Yours truly,
Miss Colson

She had not made any mistakes—unless the entire letter was a mistake. When she pulled the paper from the typewriter, Breanna made a beeline to her. She read it.

"No, Mary Ellen. If I send that, he will think I'm some stiff old prude like. . .like Uncle Harv."

Mary Ellen thought she was about to say *like you*. After all, Breanna had already accused her of being like Uncle Harv.

"What would you say?"

"Dear Sweetheart." Breanna giggled.

Mary Ellen closed her eyes and shook her head.

"Okay." Breanna conceded, seeming to think Mary Ellen would never be so bold or so flighty. "Now, type what I dictate."

Mary Ellen typed as her sister dictated.

"Not bad," she said when Breanna finished. That's what Mary Ellen would liked to have written. "Let's add the words *the Lord willing*."

Breanna's face screwed up. "The Lord willing?"

"He said he was a moral person. How can you be moral if you're not a Christian? That will let him know you're no heathen."

"I want to do this, Mary Ellen. And I prayed about it. See, I'm not completely a lost cause."

Mary Ellen felt a twinge of guilt. No, Breanna was a good girl. She studied hard and did the work assigned to her. So she fancied a more romantic life. Wasn't that better than deciding she may never have one?

The time had come for her sister to spread her wings. She had to reach out for life. Maybe what she dreamed of didn't exist in Hawaii.

But maybe it didn't exist in San Francisco either.

Mary Ellen felt as if she'd just lost a sweetheart, nevertheless she said, "You won't be able to do this without Uncle Harv's approval. Let's make this legitimate, and see if he can get you a job at the immigration office in Hawaii. If you're still determined after you've finished the school year and turn eighteen, I'll give you the money for the trip."

Breanna threw her arms around Mary Ellen's shoulders. "I love you, Mellie. And when I get to Hawaii, I can turn down the marriage proposal if I don't like the man. But I do want your blessing."

"If this works out for you," Mary Ellen said, letting Breanna know she wanted her to be happy, "I'll make your wedding dress for you."

three

Mary Ellen approached Uncle Harv the morning after the letter had been typed to Mr. C. She hadn't mailed it, wanting to make sure Breanna would not be alone in Hawaii with only a photo as her means of self-preservation.

"Uncle Harv." She set his cup of tea in front of him. "Could I talk with you. . .personally?"

"Of course, my dear." But he seemed quite surprised when she rolled her chair over to his desk. He moved his cup and saucer aside, took off his glasses, folded his hands in front of him, and gazed at her.

His face looked younger and even handsome without his glasses. Had he removed them to see her better or not to see her at all? But he was making an effort to listen.

She reminded him that he'd said the immigration office in Hawaii would be glad to hire someone from the United States.

"Yes, and I thought you might be considering such a change." He unclasped his hands and laid the palms flat on his desk. "You have every right."

Surprised at his discernment, Mary Ellen stared at his hands toying with his glasses. He focused again on her. "I know Hawaii is appealing, and I'm afraid my descriptions have made it so."

She realized for the first time that his blue eyes resembled her mother's eyes, which many people said were like hers and Breanna's.

The similarity gave her a warm feeling for him. He began saying how much he had appreciated her work. "Although it's been over four years since the earthquake and fires that destroyed so many records, there is still work to be done in

23

that area. You've been invaluable to this office."

That touched her. "Uncle Harv, it's Breanna who wants to make the trip to Hawaii."

He looked dumbfounded. "I thought you—"

"Breanna is intent upon this."

The look of relief on his face prompted her to speak further of Breanna's determination to leave when she reached the age of eighteen.

He nodded as she spoke, then gave his opinion. "Her work experience is limited. But she does speak English and she can file." Putting his hand to his mouth, he cleared his throat. "I could recommend her for the Hawaii office. If they accept her, then the office will pay her passage."

Oh no. If it were discovered there had been a deception and Breanna's reason for going to Hawaii was Mr. C.'s photo, there could be trouble for Uncle Harv, Breanna, even Mr. C., and herself. The authorities might take control.

"No, Uncle Harv. Please let me pay Breanna's passage. I have been against her leaving. If I do this, it will show her I'm not angry. Things will be right with us again."

"Oh, she's not the kind of girl to be angry with anyone."

"Not angry, no. But hurt."

"Maybe I should pay—"

"Oh, Uncle," she interrupted, not really knowing what he was about to say. "Her passage could be your going-away gift to her. And her birthday present."

"Yes," he said. "I like seeing her here. She is a breath of fresh air, although sometimes it seems she is more like a storm brewing. I've never paid her much"—he drew in a deep breath—"money or attention. I just—"

"Oh, we know you love us, Uncle Harv. We agreed the best place for Breanna was at the orphanage instead of with you, since you had no wife."

"You were good to work at the orphanage so you could be near her."

"You visited." He had made monthly visits to ensure they

were cared for properly. "But she would be so grateful for you to pay her passage and give your blessing."

"You think so?"

"Yes. And so would I."

He lifted a hand. "Done. I'll book her passage on the best liner and find someone to watch over her."

She would like to hug him, mainly for this personal talk. However, he slipped the glasses over his eyes and slid his cup in front of him.

"Thank you, Uncle Harv. Let me get you some hot tea." She reached for his cup.

"Thank *you*." He stared at the papers on his desk. For some strange reason she thought he was thanking her for something other than a cup of hot tea.

&

Hilo, Hawaii, one week later

"Any general delivery for Mr. C.?" He'd asked that for the past three days, although a carrier pigeon couldn't get a letter there so soon.

Now a week had passed from when the letter would have arrived in San Francisco. The clerk searched a stack and pulled out an envelope. That was it. A letter with the San Francisco postmark. He put that on top of Honeycutt mail he'd take to the office later.

He walked up the street to a restaurant and ordered a knife and a cup of coffee. His instinct was to rip it open, yet another part of him was concerned about what he'd find inside.

The waitress's stare questioned him. But he supposed not many people ordered a knife along with their coffee—and he'd asked that the knife be brought right away.

She brought it, laid it on the table, and took a step back.

He'd seen Akemi and other workers slice open envelopes with one quick movement. It didn't work that way for him, and he didn't like the little jagged edges he was making.

"Want me to do that for you?" The waitress was more amiable now that she saw his purpose for the knife.

"Please." His palms were sweaty.

She opened the envelope effortlessly and returned it, but took the knife away.

He felt the envelope. There seemed to be something like a photo in it, but maybe that was wishful thinking. He peeked inside. Okay. But the letter first. He laid the photo face down and read the letter:

> *Dear Mr. C.,*
> *Your photo arrived at the immigration office. If you're serious, I'm interested. I am planning a trip to Hawaii within a few weeks to the immigration office to be exact, where I expect to be offered a job.*
> *I shall be glad to speak with you, the Lord willing.*
> *I look forward to your reply.*
>
> *Yours truly,*
> *Miss B. Colson*
> *Immigration Office*
> *San Francisco, California USA*

His thoughts trembled. His elation turned to suspicion. Miss B. probably worked at the San Francisco office since she now had a job in Hawaii. The immigration office wouldn't normally hire someone sight-unseen and without references.

The waitress brought his coffee, and his mind conjured up new possibilities. Maybe she was a middle-aged spinster. If she was part of that office, she might have a way of making him marry her even if he wasn't pleased or if she was too old. Until now, he hadn't thought about the negative aspects. She didn't mention being blond. If this was legitimate, she was fat and ugly.

Why would any decent-looking America woman travel this far to meet him? Was she desperate? Was this God's will, or was she some kind of prudish religious fanatic by saying *if the Lord was willing*?

Why?

Why? He emitted a short laugh.

The photo.

That's why.

With that, his mind eased, and he slowly turned over the photo. It took his breath away.

No, he mustn't touch that coffee cup. He would surely spill it. His hand might never stop shaking. There was the most beautiful girl in the world. More beautiful than the widely acclaimed Akemi.

Miss B.

I am in love.

And I must do everything in my power to keep you from going to the immigration office before we talk.

A few weeks. Yes! He would reply immediately.

His mind came alive with plans.

Just as quickly, a new fear arose.

What if she misrepresented herself as some Japanese men had done in seeking a picture bride?

What if she turned out to be nothing like the beauty in the photo?

What if she was thinking the same thing about him?

four

Mary Ellen held out the letter addressed to Miss B. Her sister squealed like a greased pig at the county fair caught by its hind legs.

Breanna had known at least a week would pass before a letter reached Hawaii, and another week for a reply to reach San Francisco. Nevertheless, she moaned that it was the longest two weeks of her life. She lived and breathed for a letter from Hawaii.

The thought occurred to Mary Ellen that Mr. C. might reply that Breanna looked much too young for him and ask if she had an older sister. But she knew that wouldn't happen.

Breanna's words confirmed that as soon as she began to read the letter. "He thinks I'm the most beautiful woman in the whole world."

Mary Ellen hoped her reply would not be perceived as jealousy. "There's no doubt about your looks, Breanna. Or his, judging by that photo. But building a life with someone takes more than having an appealing outer appearance."

Breanna spoke seriously. "But without something to excite you about another person, wouldn't marriage be like. . .just another job?"

Mary Ellen supposed she had a point. Breanna slumped into a chair as if the words in that letter weakened her knees. A few ahs and oohs escaped her throat while she held what appeared to be another photo. Finally, she clutched the letter and photo to her chest. "You can stop worrying. This is much deeper than how he looks. His words are touching my heart."

What did a man like Mr. C. say to touch a woman's heart?

She waited. But Breanna did not share what the man of her dreams had written. Looking at the contemplative, secretive smile on her sister's face, Mary Ellen suspected her sister had, seemingly overnight, become a young woman.

Mary Ellen walked to the window, feeling quite alone now that Breanna had pulled out a sheet of stationery and concentrated on what she was writing, likely a response to Mr. C.

Breanna considered Mary Ellen as having lived in the dark ages. And in a way, she had. Candles and oil lamps were becoming a thing of the past. One could now walk at night without a lantern. In the city, gaslights bordered the streets, and electric lights shone from the windows of many homes.

Life was moving at a fast pace. When Mary Ellen was Breanna's age, horses were the main mode of transportation. Now cable cars were full of passengers. Buses and automobiles were fast replacing horses. Her own life seemed to be at a standstill. But she should be thankful. She had prayed that Breanna would enjoy her young life. It seemed that her prayer was being answered.

The Hilo immigration office sent a letter from Mr. Hammeur, assuring Uncle Harv that the recommendation from him was well received and a position would be made available for his niece.

"That's nice," Breanna said when Mary Ellen told her, as if she were speaking of a typical sunny day and not what might keep her in the necessities of life.

Uncle Harv began to spend more time in the office, and he talked more. He spoke of the time, not too many years ago, when the passage to Hawaii from San Francisco took at least five months. Now, the voyage could be made in five days, or a week at the most.

The days seemed to be passing as quickly as those steamboats he talked about plowing across the ocean. Breanna's time was taken up with school, planning what she would pack for the trip, and writing letters to Mr. C., who sent one or two letters a week. She said he was describing Hawaii and telling all about himself. But she did not share those details with Mary Ellen.

Uncle Harv booked passage for the day after Breanna's eighteenth birthday and contacted a middle-aged couple who had booked passage at the same time. They expressed delight at functioning as Breanna's guardians on the voyage.

Single young men at church expressed disappointment that lovely Breanna would be leaving to work in Hawaii, which sounded so permanent. The young women wanted to accompany her. Mary Ellen didn't say so, but so did she.

Mr. Frank disapproved when Mary Ellen told him of her need to make a withdrawal. Being her financial adviser, he had every right to express his opinion. "It's your money, of course," Mr. Frank said. "But this is a large amount."

She told him about Breanna's new job in Hawaii. He wasn't pleased. "She has badgered me for her money for at least two years. I hope you aren't going to let her waste yours. You planned to buy a home together, and you've been faithful to add to your account monthly." He scoffed. "She has never added one penny."

"She works only a few hours a week," Mary Ellen said in defense of her sister. "She contributes to our well-being."

"Yes." His eyes rolled like he didn't believe a word of it.

"She's just a child, Mr. Frank."

"Yes. And that child is off to Hawaii alone?"

Mary Ellen could have asked who could stop her. Instead, she said, "Breanna is almost eighteen."

His yes sounded like a moan. "I've been eighteen, believe it or not, and had two boys who were in that dastardly state of being." He mumbled, "Still are, if you ask me." But he wrote her check. "Here you are. It's your money."

Their gazes held. He seemed to be saying it had just become Breanna's money. But a sister had an obligation to make sure her younger sister had enough money to live on until she could earn a wage in Hawaii.

Mary Ellen needed to give Breanna both a birthday and going-away present. And as an expression of her blessing, she would make the most beautiful wedding dress in the world for the world's most attractive couple.

Finally, the day arrived when Mary Ellen and Uncle Harv stood on the dock and waved good-bye to Breanna. All too soon, the steamship disappeared into the horizon.

The days passed slowly, and Mary Ellen knew firsthand how Breanna had felt while waiting for a letter from the island.

Two weeks after Breanna's departure, Mary Ellen could share with Uncle Harv that a postcard had arrived:

Dear Mary Ellen,
Arrived today. All is better than I expected. Not working at the immigration office.
Don't worry if I don't write for a while. Getting settled. And I won't marry without you here.
My best to Uncle Harv.
Thank you both again.

I love you, Breanna

Mary Ellen felt like she'd been holding her breath until a message came. Uncle Harv was pleased, too, but concerned. "Does that mean she is not working at the office yet? Or not planning to?"

A shrug was all she could offer him. If all was well with Mr. C., he might not want his wife to work. Maybe tomorrow a long letter with details would arrive.

It didn't.

But getting settled would take time. Breanna might be looking for a job somewhere other than at the immigration office since she had enough money to live on for a while.

But she'd written that she would not marry without her sister there. Mary Ellen went shopping. The first stop was for the latest Parisian fashion magazine for the designs of the newly acclaimed Coco Chanel. At the cloth shop, she acquired materials and patterns she could modify, if necessary, to be exactly like a Parisian gown. She envisioned thousands of seed pearls on her beautiful sister's wedding gown.

The following day, Uncle Harv frowned when he read the letter from the Hawaiian immigration office. "It's been three weeks since she arrived in Hilo," he said. "But she still has not reported to the office."

"Then her remark on the postcard meant she did not intend to work at the immigration office. Or being adventurous like she is, she will want to see the sights of Hawaii you've talked about."

"I suppose."

A week later, no further word had come from Hawaii. Something didn't feel right. What was Breanna doing?

There was one way to find out.

Mary Ellen decided Breanna needed her more than Uncle Harv did. She dreaded having to tell him.

"Uncle Harv. I must go to Hawaii."

He shocked her by saying, "I'm not surprised."

On the second day of the voyage, the long, elegant steamship seemed like no more than a flyspeck on a vast ocean that could be swallowed up in hungry, chomping waves. Storm clouds rolled in, and lightning split the sky. While the ocean slammed the portholes and the ship rocked, Mary Ellen prayed and tried to believe the captain and crew when they assured the passengers all was well. They would be out of the storm soon, and the ship had been through much worse. They knew the routes.

Mary Ellen shuddered to think what passengers had gone through when the trip had taken five months. Riding the waves for even one day during a storm was scary enough.

The passengers sat at tables in the dining room at meal-times, talked and laughed perhaps a little too much to cover any anxiety. The musicians played much louder than when the sea had been calm.

Mary Ellen thought of it as analogous to her feelings over the past weeks. She'd lectured herself, prayed, and tried to accept what Breanna planned to do, but her emotions had been in turmoil.

She'd met many of the passengers during the ship's welcome party the first night. Most were Americans. Although some were travelers and tourists from Europe, many were businessmen, and some were honeymooners.

Several passengers were government officials whom Uncle Harv knew personally. Mary Ellen accepted the invitation to sit at a table for meals with a family going to Honolulu on vacation. They were from England and had visited a daughter in San Francisco. The parents had two young boys and a seventeen-year-old girl named Enid.

Mary Ellen glanced questioningly at Enid, who kept moving her hand to the side of her skirt.

Finally, the girl sighed. "I have a tear in my gown. It caught on a deck chair when the wind started blowing."

"I can mend it for you." Mary Ellen had brought along her sewing equipment since there had not been time for her to finish making Breanna's dress.

By the time she'd mended the dress, they had become friends. Mary Ellen arranged the girl's hair in a becoming style, as she had done for Breanna many times.

"Your hair is such a pretty color," Enid said.

"Thank you." Mary Ellen glanced at her hair in the mirror. She'd become accustomed to wearing it in a roll above her ears and around to the back of her head. She wore jeweled combs on special occasions, which had been few.

She focused on Enid's brown hair. The girl was plain, but with a little fixing up, she presented a comely appearance. She and her parents were quite pleased with the attractive young woman Enid had become.

Sometime during the night, either the storm abated or the ship navigated out of it. The sunshine greeted them on a calm ocean, and Mary Ellen started a morning Bible study on deck.

Parents were glad to have their children involved in scripture study, and a few mothers attended. She patterned it after the Bible studies she'd helped with at the orphanage. After she and Breanna moved to the boardinghouse, Mary Ellen had kept up the practice. At the orphanage, the girls weren't allowed to question the scripture. But with Mary Ellen, Breanna had questioned almost everything, and often Mary Ellen felt she couldn't answer sufficiently.

She would soon see her darling Breanna. She'd been lonely without her. She anticipated the exuberant hugs they would exchange and the exciting Hawaiian adventures her sister would relate.

Perhaps Mr. C. would be standing there, hat in hand, his face aglow with his appreciation of Breanna. Mary Ellen would not allow her heart to beat fast as it had done when she looked at his photo. As the sea calmed, so would she. She would be the spinster sister-in-law to Mr. C. Not because she couldn't have gotten a man, but because she had put Breanna first.

"*Kala mai ia'u.*"

Mary Ellen stood with Enid at the railing, looking out over the ocean for any sight of land when the words sounded over the loudspeaker.

"This is your captain speaking. I have just wished you a good evening. My Hawaiian is limited and my pronunciation is atrocious, but I want to say your voyaging with us has been a pleasure. Farewell, until we meet again. Aloha, *a hui hou.*"

Enid shrugged. "I only see water."

"Maybe he climbed up there." Mary Ellen pointed to the sail high above them. "And has binoculars."

In a matter of moments, the deep blue of the water and sky began to turn red. Far on the horizon, a jagged dark edge emerged.

Enid gasped. "You don't think that's another volcano eruption, do you?"

"No. It's the sunset. My uncle described the sunsets as scarlet or crimson. He says the color is more brilliant and different than anywhere he's ever traveled. And he's been all over Europe. Even went to Japan when he was a boy. His parents were in the shipping business."

"Oh, people can go anywhere nowadays," Enid said. "I mean with steamship travel. And automobiles. We have one."

"Uncle Harv has one for business and one of his own."

"I guess America had telephones before we did. And electricity. That's why everybody wants to come to America." Enid sighed. "You get everything first."

"Oh no. We still don't have the English accent."

Enid laughed.

The horizon continued to rise out of the ocean as the world turned to scarlet.

By the time they docked, the red sun had dipped into the ocean, and the sky deepened to magenta. Tall trees appeared like gigantic umbrellas, protecting the island from hot sun or rain, although she'd heard rain rarely fell on most of Hawaii.

"Look." Enid pointed.

Passengers had gathered around the ship's railing, looking and waving. Mary Ellen had been told that men in canoes would meet the ship. Even in the fading sun, this was an impressive scene. Using their strong arms, bronzed men with garlands of flowers draped around their necks and down their chests rowed the canoes.

In San Francisco she might have been embarrassed to see so many men without shirts. But they looked natural—as if they fit right in with this exotic island.

"Are they wearing skirts?" Enid asked.

"Looks like it." Mary Ellen observed the red, orange, yellow, and green material wrapped around them. "But they are handsome and colorful."

"Pretty as a parrot." Enid giggled. Her eyes widened. "You think they're going to kidnap us?"

Mary Ellen glanced from the men to Enid. "We should be so lucky."

The rhythm of the oars made music with the water, and the canoes formed paths of white-tipped furrows on the ocean. When they neared the ship, they lifted their oars and shouted, "Aloha. *Komo mai*." They turned in unison and led the ship into dock.

Ahead on the beach stood men, women, and children dressed in colorful clothes and flowered necklaces.

When Enid and her family bade her good-bye, Mary Ellen assured them that her sister would meet her. As she walked down the gangplank, she tried to take in the scene around her while remaining on the lookout for Breanna. Greetings and welcomes began from the moment passengers' feet touched the white sandy beach.

She felt bombarded with music, greetings, and conversations. Some women carrying colorful leis and wearing white blouses and flowered skirts were telling others they were from the tourism company. She didn't see Breanna. But the beach was crowded with welcomers, passengers, crew members taking baggage off the ship, and men at the dock coming forward to help.

Maybe she should have contacted someone, perhaps the tourism company. She had felt it useless to send a letter to the immigration office since Breanna had written she was not working there. Mary Ellen sent her letters to C. Honeycutt at general delivery, that being her one way of contacting her sister.

She scanned the crowd. Breanna should be rushing toward her. She should have gotten the message.

Trying to dispel her growing anxiety, she focused on the music, flowers, laughter, anything that spoke of her having landed in a magical place.

The crowd, however, was dwindling. Palms swayed in the chilly breeze. Shadows were moving in.

But her sister was nowhere in sight.

five

"Aloha, my dear. Welcome to Hawaii," said a pleasant female voice. Oh my, the sun had set but it seemed to have risen in this woman. The coppery-red hair was akin to that sunset, and her eyes even in this creeping twilight were as green as the pictures of Hawaii's famous grasses.

Mary Ellen looked into the face of a lovely, exuberant woman, maybe around sixty years old, dressed like a stylish San Francisco woman. The lovely, elegant woman with her smiled, said aloha, and draped a flowered lei over Mary Ellen's head.

"I'm Matilda," the colorful woman said, "and this is Rose. We help with the tourism office, but we are not official greeters. We're just your friendly, everyday persons who want you to feel at home and make sure things go as you expect here."

If she represented an everyday woman, then Hawaii's advertisements didn't do it justice. "Thank you." Mary Ellen felt like she was among friends.

"Are you expecting someone to meet you?" Rose said. "We know everyone and everything around here."

"My sister, Breanna Colson. I haven't received a letter from her in a while, but I wrote to say I was coming. Maybe she was delayed."

"Breanna Colson." Matilda glanced at Rose, who didn't offer any information. Their lack of knowledge about her sister seemed to indicate there were some things they didn't know.

"She's younger than I. She's eighteen. We resemble each other—coloring and everything—but she's prettier."

Matilda scoffed. "I can't imagine any girl prettier than you."

37

Rose nodded agreement.

That confirmed it. They hadn't seen Breanna.

"Do you have an address," Rose said, "or some way to contact her?"

Mary Ellen hesitated, not wanting to say the name of the man in the photo. He might not take kindly to her revealing he advertised for a bride. "I sent my letters to general delivery at Hilo Post Office."

Matilda waved. "This may be as simple as her not picking up her mail."

"My uncle sent a letter to the Hilo immigration office, and they offered her a job. She helped out in the San Francisco office. Uncle Harv is an official. He—"

"Harv?" Matilda squealed. "Not Harv Skidmore."

Mary Ellen nodded but wondered if Matilda thought that was good or bad.

Rose punched Matilda's arm. "The same Harv Skidmore we did the town with? Yes. He was from San Fran."

"Exactly," Matilda said. "Oh, we had some grand nights."

Mary Ellen was dumbfounded. Uncle Harv struck her as being rather stodgy. She couldn't imagine him doing the town. On the other hand, she could imagine these women doing it—whatever it entailed.

"You said she's working at the immigration office?"

"She wrote that she didn't take the job. I haven't heard from her in several weeks." Oh, how could this have happened?

As if she didn't know. It happened because of a photo of a handsome man with daring eyes.

"I don't know where to go, what to do—"

"Fluff and feathers," Matilda said. "You know us. Now, how long has your sister been here?"

"A little more than six weeks."

Despite the many sounds around them, a silence seemed to settle. Then Matilda, in her positive tone of voice, reasoned aloud. "You said she didn't take the job at the immigration office. She might have gone to another of our islands. She could be on a boat that's running late. Don't worry. If she doesn't show up in a little while, you can come with us. We'll leave word around here that she's expected, and they can tell her to come to our place."

"Your place?"

"The Matti-Rose Inn."

She breathed easier, hearing the name of the inn Uncle Harv had spoken about. Maybe he *had* done the town with these two.

"We live in a house near the inn," Matilda said. "We like to be near town so we can know everything that goes on."

Mary Ellen was reluctant to say it, but she must. "But you don't know anything about my sister?"

"That means," Rose said quickly, "if anything troubling had happened, we would know about it. This is just some misunderstanding."

"Come home with us." Matilda smiled and touched her arm. "Tomorrow, we can decide what to do. But first, let's ask around the docks." She called, "Billy! Jack!" A young man and a muscular middle-aged man looked around. She motioned, and they hurried to them. Matilda asked if they'd seen a pretty young blond woman in the past couple of months or so. "She would look something like this one."

Mary Ellen thought, judging from their broad smiles, they maybe looked at her a little too long.

While they appraised her, Matilda explained. "Blonds always attract attention because so many Asians with dark hair are arriving constantly."

"You mean the picture brides?"

Both women nodded.

The men said they didn't remember anyone that fit Breanna's description.

"If you see a blond, tell her to come to the reverend's house or the Matti-Rose."

"Yes, ma'am," the older man said. "You want us to get her baggage?"

At Matilda's questioning glance, Mary Ellen nodded and pointed out which were her bags and trunk.

The men apparently knew the nearby wagon belonged to these women. They thrust her bags into it, and both hefted her trunk up beside them.

Matilda drew out a change purse from which she took a couple of gold coins. Their eyes grew as wide as their smiles. "I can take these to the Matti-Rose, if you want me to," the younger one said.

"Take us all to the reverend's house, Billy."

The young man jumped up onto the wagon seat and grabbed the reins. Mary Ellen followed Matilda and Rose as they stepped up into the wagon, and the three of them sat behind Billy. He flicked the reins, gave a command, and off the horse trotted away from the dock and along the street of a small town.

Mary Ellen saw no cars, but many people walked along the sidewalks. Matilda and Rose pointed out businesses and restaurants.

After they'd traveled not more than a half mile, the huge moon hung low in the sky, giving a soft yellow glow to the muted green grass, thick foliage, and tall palm trees.

"One of you is married to a reverend?" Mary Ellen said.

"No, dear. Rose and I have too much to do and too many places in the world to visit instead of taking on a man to tie us down."

"I was married for many years," Rose said. "I value those times, but now Matilda and I do as we please."

"The reverend was my brother," Matilda said. "He died a few years ago. Rose and I decided to stay here, renovate a little, get some electricity and a refrigerator. You could stay at the inn, but I think you'll enjoy being with us instead of where you have to traipse down the hall for a hot bath."

"That settles it. A hot bath would be heaven. But I've heard so many different stories. I wasn't sure what kind of facilities might be here. Even in San Francisco, many people have had electricity and phones and modern conveniences for only a few years."

"Oh, we know, dear," Matilda said. "Rose and I have traveled throughout Europe and the U.S. You see, I'm from Texas, and Rose is from Scotland."

Soon Billy drove up to a charming, two-story, white clapboard house surrounded by thick foliage. He jumped down and slid the trunk down a board he took from the back of the wagon. Matilda took the leather handle on one side of the trunk and the two of them carried it up the steps, across the porch, and into the house.

"Let's just take these upstairs," Matilda said to Billy.

Mary Ellen and Rose followed with the other bags into a bedroom.

"Here you are." Matilda withdrew another gold coin and flipped it to Billy. He caught it as if he were accustomed to the game. He and Rose went downstairs.

"Freshen up if you need to," Matilda told her. "Then we'll trot over to the inn."

In the bathroom, Mary Ellen looked longingly at the claw-foot bathtub, but settled for washing her hands, splashing cold water on her face, and drying with the hand towel.

Returning to the bedroom, her attention was drawn to the trunk. She unfastened the leather straps and took a key from her purse and unlocked it. She removed the large bundle wrapped in tissue paper and laid it on the bed.

She carefully unrolled it, held it up to her, and walked to the mirror. She imagined the man in the photo standing next to the dress. He was in a black tux, standing tall and having the darkest hair and most brilliant eyes she'd ever seen. His straight nose and full lips made a perfect picture.

How much more appealing would he be in person? Breanna would be breathtakingly beautiful in the white dress. She could almost see the two of them together in front of the preacher, saying their vows.

"Mary Ellen?"

Her mouth opened and her eyes widened to see not Mr. C. standing beside her in the mirror, but Matilda.

"Oh."

&

"I didn't mean to startle you." Matilda touched the dress. "This is beautiful. Are you to be married?"

"It's for Breanna. For when she marries. I haven't finished it yet."

Matilda looked astounded. "You made this?"

"Yes. I took sewing in school and worked as the orphanage seamstress while Breanna was there. I thought we should be together, since we lost our parents."

"You've given up your life for her, haven't you, dear?"

"I didn't really have anything to give up. We lost everything in the earthquake and fire." She drew in a shaky breath. "Breanna and I are. . .family."

"What about your uncle?"

"It was comforting to know we had an uncle. But the relationship was really just a working one. He's a bachelor, set in his ways, and didn't want any females disrupting his life." She was quick to add. "But he always tried to do right by us. He just didn't know how to relate." She smiled. "Breanna came close to drawing him out of his shell. She's so appealing."

After a moment of thoughtfulness, Matilda smiled. "Consider me and Rose your family. We're here for you."

Mary Ellen had trouble keeping back the moisture that threatened her eyes when Matilda reached out and gently touched her cheek. She wished Breanna had met Matilda and Rose on her arrival.

As they trotted across the street and down the sidewalk, Matilda said, "Did your sister come to meet a man?"

Mary Ellen couldn't fathom why she would ask that, but she spoke truthfully. "Yes. She did."

When both women smiled, she said, "What?"

"Oh," Matilda said. "I'm just thinking about when I was eighteen. If a particular man were involved, I, too, might be delayed in meeting my sister. In fact, there was a span of ten years when I didn't see my brother. I loved him. But I was. . . occupied."

Mary Ellen thought of Mr. C.'s photo.

Before that, she would not have understood.

"This used to be the mission school," Matilda said when they stood in front of a two-story, white clapboard building. The upper and lower porches were surrounded by banisters. Light blue shutters flanked each side of the windows. A lava stone walkway was bordered by flowers and bushes that appeared to grow wild and natural.

Before they went inside, Matilda told her about Akemi, a girl who had traveled from Japan three years ago to become a picture bride when she was sixteen years old. "The man lied to her, so we could not let the marriage take place. She helps at the inn."

"She also works at the immigration office part-time," Rose said. "She might know if your sister went there."

They found Akemi in the kitchen. Mary Ellen was struck by the girl's beautiful fair face surrounded by straight black hair. Her dark eyes reflected the same friendliness as her smile.

Akemi bowed.

"Please. You don't need to bow to me."

"Oh, Miss Matilda and Miss Rose tell me that all the time. But I forget. I just naturally do it. Like you shake hands."

"Then it's okay."

Akemi made them each a cup of tea.

Mary Ellen took a picture from her pocket and handed it to Akemi. "My sister might have gone to the immigration office."

Akemi smiled. "She pretty like you." Then her face saddened. "Mr. Hammeur say American woman come work with us. But I no see her. If she come to the office, I remember." She shook her head. "Sorry my English not good."

"You speak fine. I understood."

"She's very smart," Matilda said. "Working part-time at the immigration office, helping at the inn, and taking a few classes at school."

Akemi smiled shyly. "I try. Maybe your sister come when I away from office."

Mary Ellen didn't like seeing the sadness on Akemi's face. "Maybe she didn't go to the office. She decided not to work there. She's. . .headstrong."

"Oh, we identify with that, don't we, Rose?" Matilda said.

Rose laughed. "Even more so after I became acquainted with Matilda. But don't you worry. If your sister comes tonight after you're asleep, we will wake you."

Mary Ellen tried to dismiss the word *if* from her mind.

"We will check at the office in the morning, just in case. But your young, headstrong sister is probably. . ." Matilda waved her hand. "Having a fling."

Mary Ellen grimaced and Matilda patted her hand. "A nice fling."

That could be.

Or not.

"You said, *we* will check in the morning?"

"Oh yes. We can't let you traipse around alone. Besides, this is too juicy to pass up. I'm dying of curiosity. You see, I've been young."

Mary Ellen had a feeling Matilda still was, except chronologically, and with her, it didn't seem to matter.

"When I came here, twenty-something years ago, my adventurous niece and her companion came, too."

Rose smiled. "Her niece, Jane, married my son, Mak, who owns the cattle ranch a few miles from here."

"Oh, the good times we had," Matilda said. "Racing horses, visiting royalty. Those were the days. Now," she said. "We've become a part of the United States."

The way she said that made Mary Ellen wonder if she thought that was good or bad. Finding out might be interesting.

Being adventurous, headstrong, and impulsive began to have an appeal to Mary Ellen. For someone like Matilda, Rose, Jane, and. . .Breanna.

૨ઠ

Early the next morning after a good night's sleep at the house, Mary Ellen dressed in the clothes she'd taken from her trunk the night before. She had followed instructions on how to pack and had rolled her outerwear around her underclothes which prevented excessive wrinkling.

She wore light lipstick and her usual practical hairstyle, a tailored dark skirt, and a white blouse, wanting to give every impression she meant business when she asked about her sister.

Matilda and Rose also dressed in skirts and blouses, but entirely different from hers. Matilda's was a brightly flowered skirt against a green background and a grass-green blouse. Rose wore a slim burgundy skirt with a burgundy-trimmed pink blouse.

Those women would certainly stand out in any crowd, especially the exuberant Matilda with her copper-colored hair and green eyes.

"We'll take the automobile, since we have time before the office opens. If we were late, we'd take the horse and carriage. We'd get there quicker."

"Those autos can be more stubborn than a mule—just refuse to move," Rose said. "And a flick of a whip makes no difference at all."

Mary Ellen climbed into the backseat of the car. On the street were a few men on horses, a couple of carriages, and several wagons. "Are there many autos here?"

"Last I heard," Rose said, "there were three. But there are seventy or more in Oahu."

Matilda drove across the way to the Matti-Rose. Akemi came out as soon as the car stopped, but Matilda tooted the *chaooooga*-sounding horn anyway.

"That's a beautiful kimono," Mary Ellen said as Akemi

climbed into the back beside her.

"Thank you. Most days I wear Japanese dress."

As soon as Matilda swerved out into the road, she tooted her horn loudly at a man on a horse in the road. She shouted out the window. "An auto can't move sideways. Get that animal out of the road before I run over it."

"Now 'Tilda, settle down," the man said. "You're gonna cause this mare to sprint and run away, and you'll be responsible for my death."

"Well, you won't be around to complain about it. Now move it."

He laughed, tipped his hat, and galloped on.

"That's ol' Scooter. Works down at the docks. He thinks I'm joking when I say things like that."

Mary Ellen didn't. Even in this short period of time, she figured Matilda would barrel down the road and anyone in the way had better move or else. Rose just smiled pleasantly, as if everything was normal.

six

"Mmmhmm," Lalani hummed. She set a cup of Kona coffee on the table without his having to order it.

The middle-aged waitress had told him time and again, "Claybourne Honeycutt, you have the perfect name for a man like you. You're a honey if ever I saw one. Mmmhmm." She'd shake her head and grin, then hold out her hand. "If it wasn't for this ring, and my husband having killer instincts, and my being twenty years too late, I'd do the town with you, honey."

Lalani had said that since before he'd turned sixteen and had finally condensed it to "Mmmhmm" and a grin.

He took a big gulp of the steamy coffee and hoped it would give him the lift he needed before breakfast and the questionable conversation he'd enter into soon—one that would not be with Lalani.

"I heard your kind of woman arrived last night," she said. "Some of the dockworkers were saying there was another one for Clay." She raised her eyebrows. "They wouldn't dare call you *honey*." She laughed.

Clay didn't. "They weren't disrespectful about her, were they?"

"They know better after those fights you've had. We don't allow that kind of talk in here any more than you do."

Lalani looked around, as if someone might be listening. She leaned forward. "They were talking about a beautiful blond and said you'd want to know. Now, doesn't that whet your appetite?"

His appetite wasn't whetted as much as it had been when the game had started a few years ago. "This morning, I have an appetite for breakfast. But I'll settle for coffee until Jacob shows up."

"Oh, you gonna get yourself converted by that Bible-thumping preacher-boy?"

Clay forced a small laugh before taking another drink of coffee. Apparently, she couldn't tell his conversion had happened when he was a lad of nine years old. Was baptized in the ocean. Pastor Russell had said his sins were taken away farther than the eye could see on those waves. At that time, he hardly knew what sin was.

Lalani apparently took his laugh to mean *not a chance*. He set his cup down, and she refilled it.

"Jacob's not a preacher yet, Lalani. At least, not officially."

"Well, look who just walked in."

Lalani greeted the tall, lean man. "Aloha *kakahiaka*, Jacob."

Jacob answered with the same respectful, "Good morning, Lalani." He asked how she was and about her family, something Clay hadn't gotten around to. "Coffee, please," he said at last.

For the first time since he'd begun to play the game, Clay wondered if what he'd done had been perceived as fun or as a tainting of his reputation.

Jacob touched his shoulder. "Been a while, Clay." He took the seat across from him.

Clay acknowledged him with a nod. They'd grown up together—in church, in school. Had been baptized together that Sunday afternoon in the ocean. Later in high school, they'd noticed the girls, surfed, raced on the MacCauley ranch, run through the sugarcane fields, enjoyed being young. Then came a time of growing up. After getting higher education in Europe, Clay went into the sugar business with his family. Jacob became a teacher, specializing in Bible studies.

There was still a bond between them. But they now had their different interests and ways of life. Just as whaling had once been, and then cattle ranching, sugar was now Hawaii's biggest product, sent all over the world, and Clay took seriously his responsibilities in the Honeycutt Sugar Company.

But that's not what separated him and Jacob. Several years

before, Jacob had fallen in love, but his girlfriend had gone to Europe to study. While there, she married a Scotsman. Jacob tried to absolve his grief by denying it. Clay had been sorry about his loss, but glad to have a friend who also enjoyed taking girls out on dates and showing them the sights of Hawaii.

The last time he and Jacob had had a serious talk, Jacob had said he himself needed to accept that his former girlfriend was not the one God had chosen for him and that he felt it was time he and Clay settled down and took life more seriously.

Clay had scoffed. "You have no right to tell me how to live my life."

"Sure I do," Jacob said, "because we're friends and I love you."

There had been nothing more to say. After a long silence, Jacob had stood, clasped Clay's shoulder, and walked away.

After that, Jacob's younger brother had taken his place in joining Clay in this game of life.

Now Jacob had walked into the restaurant, again laid his hand on Clay's shoulder for a moment, and taken a seat across from him.

Maybe Jacob wanted them to be close again. Or perhaps he needed Clay's help in some way. A donation to some charitable event. Clay would like that. It's not like he was a heathen. He simply chose the single life, which included beautiful women.

Lalani brought Jacob's coffee. "You ready to order?"

Clay liked the Portuguese sausage. He ordered it, along with two fried eggs, white rice, and guava juice.

"Sounds good to me," Jacob said, giving Clay the impression his friend had something specific on his mind.

Jacob opened the conversation by talking about what each of them had been doing. After Lalani brought their meal and Jacob asked the blessing, Jacob continued along the same line.

"Looks like the sugar business is booming, judging by

the new mills and the workers that keep swarming in from Japan."

"Honeycutt Sugar has become Hawaii's biggest export," Clay responded. "I guess we're known throughout the world. We export the sugar and import the workers."

"You did a good thing, Clay, making those strict rules about the Japanese workers being honest with the brides they're having come over to marry them."

"I can't take a lot of credit for that. Matilda and Rose brought it to my attention after Akemi was so upset and felt she had no recourse but to marry the dishonest man." He shrugged. "They made me realize a lot of other picture brides could have been in similar situations but were afraid to speak out about it. I do care what happens on the plantation."

"Your taking a personal interest will keep a lot of those young girls from thinking their only recourse from marrying a man they don't want is going into those houses of ill repute."

"I don't like that anymore than you, Jacob."

"I know that. I know you."

Clay wasn't sure where this might be leading. Could be negative or positive. He was grateful Lalani chose that moment to refill their cups.

Jacob poured milk into his coffee and stirred slowly.

Clay watched him over the rim of his glass of guava juice. Waiting.

"I have a favor to ask."

"Sure, Jacob. If I can help with anything."

Jacob's intense gaze held Clay's. "I want you to look after Geoffrey."

Clay feared the piece of Portuguese sausage he'd popped in his mouth might just cause a problem. For a moment, he wasn't able to chew. Jacob focused on his plate and cut several pieces of sausage. After a long moment of trying to figure out if Jacob was being serious or had lost his mind, he chewed slowly, then swallowed.

"Jacob, Geoffrey is twenty-five years old."

Jacob glanced across at him. "But you're twenty-nine and have a huge influence on him."

Was Jacob saying Clay was a bad influence? "You're his brother."

"You're implying," Jacob said, "I'm the one who should be a good influence on Geoffrey."

Clay shrugged one shoulder, indicating that's exactly what he meant.

"Who listens to his brother?" Jacob shook his head. "But I'm saying this because I am his brother."

Clay shrugged both shoulders. "He got his college degree. He's a good worker, Jacob. He's just trying to figure out where he belongs and what he wants—"

Jacob held up his fork. "I know all that, Clay. No need to get defensive. I haven't said a thing to condemn you or Geoffrey. You make your own choices like I make mine, and they haven't always been right."

"Okay, what do you want me to do with Geoffrey?"

"Continue to befriend him. See that he's okay." He paused. "I'm not going to be around."

"What do you mean? Are you ill?"

"No. God is leading me into the ministry. I've applied to a seminary on the mainland to get my doctorate."

That didn't surprise Clay. "When do you go?"

"The semester starts in September. Less than two months. I'd like to spend some time with my parents before I go. And with Geoffrey, if he will."

Lalani appeared with the coffeepot. Jacob said, "No thanks," but Clay accepted another refill.

"Clay, I'd like for you to come to church Sunday and bring Geoffrey. He hasn't attended in a long time."

"Sure." Clay figured he could do that. His conscience could bother him away from church as much as inside it. "If he's back on the island. Thomas needed him to train his new shipment of Japanese men."

After they finished eating, Jacob reached into his pants

pocket and brought out money to pay for the breakfast. "My treat."

Clay thanked him and picked up his cup.

Jacob spoke in a low tone. "Something else I want you to do. Let's go outside for what I have to say."

Lalani was on her way over again. Everybody knew she liked to overhear conversations and didn't mind repeating them. Jacob stood.

"I'll be in church Sunday," Lalani said. Jacob nodded and smiled.

Clay downed the rest of his coffee, and the two of them walked outside.

The morning peace was shattered with *chaoooooga-chaoooooga*.

"Sounds like Matilda." Clay laughed. He and Jacob stood on the sidewalk. "Looks like she's pulling over at the restaurant up the street. Let's find out what she's up to."

They started up the street. Matilda and Rose got out of the front seat. A blond climbed from the back. Akemi, unmistakable in her flattering kimono, exited from the other side and walked around to the sidewalk.

That must be the blond Lalani had mentioned. Clay started to pick up his pace, but Jacob turned and rushed to Clay's car. He opened the door and leaped inside.

Clay would have liked to speak to the women, particularly the blond. But they were disappearing into the restaurant. Only Matilda looked his way and lifted her hand. He did the same, then hurried to the car, wondering about Jacob's strange behavior.

Jacob's face had paled, and his gaze focused on his clenched hands.

Clay had no idea what was going on. He knew Jacob loved Matilda and Rose. What bothered him wasn't those two, although they were dynamic, hard-headed women.

Was it the blond? Did she remind him of his blond girl-friend who'd left him? Had she brought back those haunting memories of so long ago?

❧

After they were seated in the restaurant, the waitress came to the table and was introduced to Mary Ellen as Phyllis. "She was one of our school girls," Rose said, and they all smiled like that had been a pleasant experience.

"Kona for all?" Matilda asked, and they each nodded, although Mary Ellen had no idea what a *Kona* was.

"We've taught just about everybody on the island," Matilda said, as Phyllis walked away. "That is, the ones who are making good decisions. The others we don't know."

Rose laughed with her, and Akemi smiled, looking at them as if she dearly loved them.

Phyllis returned soon. "Here you are." She set four cups of brown aromatic liquid in front of each.

"Smells wonderful," Mary Ellen said. "Almost as good as the scent of flowers that seems to be everywhere."

"We are an island of flowers." Matilda smiled. "You just can't imagine the variety. But this is the world's best coffee." She added cream to hers. "It's only grown in Hawaii."

Mary Ellen took a sip. She nodded. She'd never tasted coffee so rich and good. She could drink it without the cream. But she decided the cream was probably the best in the world, too, so she picked up the little white cream pitcher.

Before long, Matilda was suggesting what Mary Ellen might like to eat. "Their specialty is macadamia nut pancakes."

"The banana are good, too," Rose said.

"Yes. And the chocolate."

"Don't forget the strawberry."

"Or blueberry."

"They're all delicious," Matilda said. "And so light and fluffy you have to set your cup on them to keep them from sprouting wings and flying away like a honeycreeper."

Phyllis giggled. "Most people keep them on the plate with a lot of our dairy-fresh whipped butter and a little powdered sugar."

"Or syrup. Oh my gracious," Matilda said. "They have a

special, fresh-fruit syrup the cooks make every day."

Phyllis was nodding. "We have maple, guava, coconut, and boysenberry today."

"Mercy." Mary Ellen laid her hand over her stomach. "I feel stuffed just hearing that."

"But of course," Phyllis said, "we have the usual breakfast foods. Eggs, meat, juices."

Mary Ellen decided. "Since I've never had macadamia pancakes, I'll have that. Oh, and bring me a honeycreeper."

She was glad to see Matilda appreciated her humor as much as she appreciated Matilda's. But she knew she was far from ever being as delightful as that colorful woman.

"All right," Matilda said. "What we normally do with a new person is order something different and then we sample everybody's. It's expected here."

The *someone new* remark turned Mary Ellen's thoughts to her sister. After Matilda said the blessing and their food was brought, they sampled each other's, but remaining in the back of Mary Ellen's mind was what might be revealed at the immigration office, where they would go after breakfast. Surely someone there had at least seen Breanna and knew how that photo had gotten into the envelope with the Japanese man's official form.

Matilda suggested they walk to the office about a half mile away. "With all the horses crowding the road, we'd have a time making our way through in that car. Besides, I just have it as a conversation piece, mainly."

As they walked, the aromas from the bakery mingled with the fresh, morning breeze, rife with the fragrance of flowers. Each restaurant emitted a new and different intriguing scent.

Before long, the unmistakable moist salty air meant they were near the dock. Soon, Mary Ellen viewed the white sand beach that spread peacefully along the ocean, fringed with green swaying palm leaves high on tall, slender tree trunks.

They walked past an impressive, four-story building that Matilda said was the Hilo Hotel. The only building in town larger than the Matti-Rose.

"I wonder if she's staying there," Mary Ellen said. "Or if she did."

Rose offered to have them check their records. "You can go on to the office. I know Akemi doesn't want to be late."

Mary Ellen, Matilda, and Akemi walked on down the sidewalk to the immigration office. Matilda opened the door, and they entered. The office in San Francisco had been in a several-story, brick building. This was one level. Light and airy. The docking area was visible from side windows. A man sat behind a waist-high partition.

"That's Mr. Hammeur," Akemi whispered.

Mr. Hammeur was a slight man with a thin nose and quick eyes. He said aloha, nodded at Akemi, and greeted Matilda warmly. When Matilda introduced her as Harvey Skidmore's niece, he took on a guarded look. "Yes, I remember Mr. Harv. Because he is a fine businessman and I respect him, I agreed to take you on, but—"

"No, that was my sister, Breanna. Did she come here about the job?"

"She did not." A furrow dented the space between his eyebrows. "I stayed late. But she did not come into the office. I did not feel it my place to inquire."

"I don't agree," Mary Ellen said. "A young woman was to take a job here, but you didn't inquire about her whereabouts?"

"I offered to hire her, sight unseen, because of the recommendation of Mr. Harv. That, already, was beyond my usual practices."

"I'm sorry," Mary Ellen said.

Mr. Hammeur exhaled a deep breath. "Your uncle did send a letter, apologizing that his niece did not take the job."

Mary Ellen could imagine that if C. Honeycutt met Breanna when she disembarked, she would have been more intrigued with him than with going to the immigration office about a job.

But so much time had passed. And these people hadn't

seen her. At least, this man *said* he hadn't. She hated being suspicious, but she needed to find her sister. "She might have been ill, or hurt."

"Now, now." Matilda touched her arm. "If anything like that had happened with an American young lady, the news would have spread. Why, it would be in the newspapers. But we will check with the hospital later."

Rose came in. "Your sister hasn't been registered at the hotel."

"Thanks for checking." She addressed Mr. Hammeur. "There is another matter."

"Yes?" He raised his eyebrows.

"Our office received correspondence from a C. Honeycutt."

"That would be Claybourne Honeycutt. The picture brides are for the Japanese men working on the Honeycutt plantation."

"I mean," she said, trying to be careful, "I got the impression from some correspondence that he was looking for an American wife."

"Looking?" He scoffed, and they all gazed at her.

"I mean someone sent his photo to our office."

"No." He shook his head vigorously. "That would not go through this office. Men like him do not advertise for a bride."

Matilda agreed. "He wouldn't need to. Women from sixteen to six—"

Rose elbowed her. Matilda grinned. "As I was saying, women from sixteen to 105 would go for Claybourne Honeycutt. Believe me, he does not need to advertise. There's some mistake, or someone is playing a practical joke."

Not too practical, Mary Ellen was thinking. *A joke was supposed to be funny.*

This was not.

Mr. Hammeur repeated his earlier words, adamantly. "Such an indiscretion could not happen through this office."

Mary Ellen nodded. "I do know that isn't the way things

are done." They all knew this Claybourne Honeycutt. If Breanna was safe with Mr. C., Mary Ellen didn't want to cause trouble for them.

"Is the job opening still available?" she asked as calmly as she could.

Mr. Hammeur was shaking his head before she finished her sentence. "After she did not arrive for two weeks, I filled the job with a young man who serves the multiple purposes of working in the office and on the dock, which had been my thought from the beginning."

"That was Billy," Matilda said. "The boy who drove us to the house last night."

Mary Ellen remembered the friendly young man who said he had not seen Breanna. But he now had the job that had been promised to her.

She was trying to force herself to believe that Breanna had not gotten her mail or was simply delayed. But the uneasiness she felt grew worse by the moment.

seven

"Did your sister come to meet Claybourne Honeycutt?"

Mary Ellen wasn't surprised that the discerning Matilda asked that question as soon as they exited the office.

"I'm afraid so."

"Now tell me exactly what was in the letter you received."

"It wasn't a letter. The photo was in the envelope with an official form from a Japanese man. The two apparently had no connection. The only information was on the back of the photo: C. Honeycutt. General delivery. Post office. Hilo, Hawaii. I'm not sure of the exact words, but he said he wanted an American wife."

She paused. "Oh yes, he wrote *occupation* and beside it he wrote *sugar plantation.*"

Matilda looked perplexed. "That young man's problem is keeping the women away from him."

"You don't think he sent the photo?"

"Well," Matilda said, "I can image he might do that, but openly. He might even go to the U.S. or anywhere and make it known he's eligible."

Mary Ellen fell in step with them as they started up the sidewalk.

Rose asked, "Was the form you received from a Japanese man who worked at the sugar plantation?"

"I think so. But I'm not sure I'd recognize the name if I saw it. Do you think a Japanese man did that to lure an American girl here?"

"No. They're well supervised. And for a Japanese man to approach a *haole* would be worse than committing the unforgivable sin."

"Hay. . . ?"

58

"Haole," Matilda said again. "That's a Caucasian or white person."

Someone sent the photo. Whether it was Mr. C. or a Japanese man, Mary Ellen didn't have a good feeling about this. She hated to say it, but she must. "Suppose Mr. Hammeur lured her here and met her."

They stared at her like she'd lost her mind. She didn't care. She had to find her sister.

"His wife would kill him," Rose said.

Matilda huffed. "She nearly does that without a reason."

"Mr. Hammeur isn't happily married?"

"Oh yes. And has five children."

"But you said—"

Matilda waved away her speculation. "She swats him with this and that, but it's all playful. He likes it."

"How well do you know Mr. Honeycutt?"

"We know the family intimately," Rose said. "Clay's grandfather and my husband were dear friends. Clay's dad and my son, Mak, were best friends. Clay's dad owned the most productive sugar plantation on this island and in Oahu." Sadness crossed her face. "Clay's parents were killed in a shipwreck." Her voice softened as she added, "Mak has been like a dad to Clay."

"And," Matilda added, "Mak owns a cattle and horse ranch. My niece Jane married him. We came here together back in 1889." She looked beyond them, as if seeing her memories. "Jane was from Texas. She won the biggest horse race Hawaii has ever seen. That's how she scared Mak to death and made him realize how much he loved her."

Rose laughed softly. "It's a great story. Jane became a hero in these parts. Those were the days of royal races."

"There's so much to tell you," Matilda said. "I know your mind is on your sister right now. But part of the reason I say everyone would know and be talking about any American woman who landed here is because Jane made American women even more famous here by winning that race. Over the king's horse, mind you. The respect for American women rose to 100 percent."

Mary Ellen let out a weighty breath. "Maybe. If Mr. C. didn't send the photo, and the sender told her Mr. C. sent him to pick her up, she might go with him."

They reached the car, and Matilda started the engine. "This is confusing. Surely no one would write for an American girl in order to do her harm. That's. . ."

She didn't finish her sentence. Had she been about to say that was insane?

Such a thought was more frightening than if the person was sane.

Matilda said. "I saw Clay's automobile when we went into the restaurant this morning, but I didn't notice if anyone was in it."

"Think about this," Rose said. "If Clay sent the photo and met her, then she is probably at his plantation. Or he's showing her the islands."

"Right," Matilda added. "I can imagine you and Clay together. So if your sister is like you've described her, he wouldn't let her out of his sight."

"But this morning. . ."

"This morning," Matilda said pointedly, "he was with Jacob. Jacob assists our pastor. Maybe Clay was talking to him about the wedding you're making that dress for."

"But would Mr. C. be that impulsive? To marry so soon after meeting—"

Before she could finish the sentence, Matilda patted Mary Ellen's hand. "Love can happen instantly. Isn't that what happened when your sister saw the photo?"

Mary Ellen whispered, "Yes." Even an ordinarily sensible person could have such a moment of weakness.

"I'll find Clay," Rose said, "and catch up with you two later."

"All right," Matilda said. "We'll go back to the house. In the meantime, Mary Ellen, would you like to see the perfect place where you can work on your sister's wedding dress?"

Mary Ellen couldn't refuse that offer. But her thoughts were a jumble. One minute, she feared something dreadful had happened to Breanna. The next, she could imagine her sister at Mr. C.'s plantation. What else could she do but let these women lead her around?

ఌ

Less than thirty minutes later, Mary Ellen could hardly believe her eyes. On the small-town street of Hilo was a shop that stood out from all the rest other than the Hilo Hotel across the street. The sign across the window read: MATTI-ROSE HAWAIIAN & WESTERN WEAR.

"The display window is beautiful. As fine as any exclusive shop I've seen in San Francisco."

"Or Europe." Matilda spoke proudly. "Rose and I love to travel and decided to make a business of it, too. Newcomers and visitors to Hawaii delight in the Hawaiian attire that's much cooler than Western wear. Native Hawaiians want everything Westerners have."

"Those are beautiful mannequins."

"The newest. These are made of papier-mâché. Only in recent years have we women shed those corsets and crinolines, so we don't need the heavy mannequins now. We carry only the more fluid lines of clothing. Oh my"—she fanned her face with her hand—"we had to have men to haul around and dress those old-fashioned wax mannequins. Their faces were ugly, too." She laughed. "I'm referring to the mannequins, not the men."

Mary Ellen laughed with her, and they entered the shop, accompanied by the tinkle of a little bell.

She met Pilar Scott, an attractive brunette who looked to be in her late thirties. "When Pilar was only seventeen, she came over with me and Jane." Matilda and Pilar smiled at each other. "I'm hoping you two will have a lot of time for conversation, but now, let Pilar see the dress you made."

Mary Ellen took it from her bag. "I still need to add the seed pearls."

"Oh, it's gorgeous," Pilar said. "And the work is expert. Matilda, have you found the new employee you've wanted?"

"Rose and I talked about that last night." She turned to Mary Ellen. "We thought you might consider helping us out here."

Mary Ellen needed time to process the offer. She had no idea how long she would be in Hawaii. How long before she found Breanna?

"That is, if you're wanting a job. While you're thinking it over, you can work on your sister's dress here. Incidentally, Pilar, have you seen Clay lately?"

Pilar shrugged. "Who can keep track of Clay?"

Matilda explained. "Clay is the younger brother of Pilar's best friend, Susanne."

Pilar shook her head. "What that *nohea haole* needs is to settle down."

Was she cursing him?

"Nohea haole," Matilda explained, "means *handsome Caucasian*."

Mary Ellen already knew if he looked anything like his photo, he was handsome. The more comments she heard about him, the more she suspected Breanna had met him and forgotten everything else. "I'll be glad to help out here. I have no way of knowing for how long."

"Let's call it temporary and part-time, if you like," Matilda said. "When would you like to start?"

This was not a time for saying she'd like to see the island. "Now?"

Matilda smiled kindly. "I thought you'd say that. Pilar can tell you all about the shop and introduce you to the workers in the back. I will return later this afternoon. And Rose will be in as soon as she learns anything. You may want to talk with Pilar about your situation. I'm sure Clay will respond to this matter right away."

Matilda laid her hand on Mary Ellen's shoulder, and her green eyes held sympathy. Mary Ellen needed to meet Mr. C., but fear of doing so must have been written all over her face.

≈

Clay looked up from the ledger when Mak knocked on the office door and walked in. "I'd like to talk with you, Clay. Could we step outside?"

"Sure thing." Clay asked his accountant to excuse him and walked away from the thundering machines inside the sugar mill.

They walked out to one of the wooden benches beneath a row of banyan trees where mill hands often ate their lunches.

"What's on your mind?" Judging by the serious look on Mak's face he must have come on business. With the tremendous influx of workers and their requested brides, Clay could barely keep up with their need for beef. His herd couldn't produce as fast as the workers and their families could consume beef, and Mak's ranch was his biggest producer. "From the expression on your face, you must either be raising your price on beef or have decided to keep that horse I want."

Mak gave him a sidelong glance. "More serious than a cow or a horse, according to Mom."

"Is she ill?" Rose was one of the most active, energetic women he knew.

"No. She asked me to talk with you about a disturbing matter. Maybe there's a simple explanation."

"A matter?" Clay couldn't think what action he'd taken that would disturb Rose.

"It's about a woman. Or I should say, a girl."

"A girl? Come on. What is this?"

Mak related the story Rose had told him, rendering Clay momentarily speechless. If it wasn't for knowing Mak MacCauley as a fine, Christian man, he'd punch him in the mouth for telling such lies.

Mak drew a deep breath. "Miss Colson thinks her sister might be with you."

Clay jumped up, and his right fist pounded his left palm. Pacing in front of Mak, he tried to absorb what his friend had said. Finally, words spouted from his lips. "That's ridiculous. You think I'd do a thing like that?"

"I only know what Mom said the woman told her and Matilda."

Clay had him run through it again, then he scoffed. "I don't have some girl stowed away. If I wanted a wife or a companion, I could have one."

"That's not the point, Clay. She claims your photo was sent to the immigration office in San Francisco, along with your name and the request for an American bride written on the back of it."

"My name?"

"Mom said she refers to you as Mr. C. Apparently you—I mean someone—wrote the name C. Honeycutt."

"I'm far from being the only Honeycutt in the world or in Hawaii, for that matter. And I didn't advertise for a wife."

"Glad to hear it. Now all you have to do is convince that woman whose sister is missing."

"Why should I bother with this nonsense?"

"Because it's not just a matter of your reputation. The woman could accuse illegal activity. . .or worse."

Clay plopped down on the bench. "Why would anyone make up such a story?"

"She said a photo of you was sent."

"But you said the photo was in an envelope with a Japanese man's official form from the Hilo immigration office." Clay scoffed. "That proves this person is lying. No Japanese man can just walk into that office and fill out a form. Any worker from my plantation would have to be accompanied by one of us in authority."

"She claims her sister came to Hawaii because of the photo, to marry you. The sister is missing."

"Missing." Clay looked at the clear blue sky over his head, then at Mak again. "You said her sister was supposed to meet her last night. This is only a half-day later. Anybody could be delayed for any reason. If the sister story is true, her horse could have gotten sick. She broke a leg. Got hit in the head with a surfboard. She could have a headache. Anything. And you said that sister is eighteen?"

"That's what Mom said."

"Frankly, I'd rather a woman be ten years older than me, not ten years younger. What in the world would I want with an eighteen-year-old?"

Mak stared at him, and Clay looked away. Finally, he shook his head. "I don't have time for this."

"You need to listen to her in case there's something to it."

"Oh, I think there's something to it. She's seen the sugar unloading at the docks in San Francisco, seen the papers where Japanese men are employed with Honeycutt Sugar, and she's looking to sweeten her life with a part of the profit."

Mak scoffed at that. "Then how did she get a photo?"

Clay sighed, thinking. "A girlfriend. Or maybe she's not telling the truth about that either. Sounds like a made-up story if I ever heard one."

"You're guessing, Clay. You don't know the facts."

"But I will. Just as soon as I tell my accountant we'll have to go over the ledgers another day. You say she's with Rose and Matilda?"

"Matilda was taking her to their dress shop."

Clay stared at Mak. "What are you grinning about?"

"Mom said she's a pretty blond. That may cool your temper."

"I've made an issue of liking blonds. But I've never lost my head or my heart to one. And don't intend to. Not some conniving one anyway."

Mak laughed.

"Now what?"

"After my first wife died, I vowed there would never be another woman in my life."

Clay watched a warmth come into his friend's eyes.

"Jane and I have been married for. . .let's see. . .about twenty years now."

Clay chuckled. "You'd better make sure. You may have an anniversary coming up. But seriously, if I found a woman like Jane, I might change my mind, too. I don't think they make many like her."

Mak smiled. "None. None at all."

Clay saw the softness come onto that tough rancher's face. He rather envied that his friend could feel that way about a woman.

Since he'd calmed down some, Clay began to think more clearly. "I appreciate your coming and talking to me." He stood and smiled at his fatherly friend. "I'll check this matter out and get it settled. I'll just bet it's not my photo at all that found its way to San Francisco. And the woman, if she's not a schemer, will know it when she sees me."

Mak nodded.

Clay watched him get on his horse and lift his hand to tip the brim of his paniolo hat in a farewell gesture and ride away.

Mak hadn't said he didn't believe the woman's story. Did he think Clay would have sent a photo and request for a woman? And why did he feel a sense of guilt when he hadn't done what he was being accused of?

Accompanied by a sense of chagrin, Clay knew if there was any truth to the story, he'd be better off to have the girl with him instead of her being missing.

eight

Mary Ellen heard the tinkling of the tiny bell and turned from the dress form to face the door. Whatever smile and greeting she'd planned stopped short. The tiny seed pearl slipped from her left hand and fell to the wooden floor. Such a small bead couldn't possibly make a sound, but it seemed to cause a roaring in her head like she'd heard when holding a seashell to her ear.

She could not think what to say. Jumbled in her mind was that Pilar had gone for sandwiches, leaving Mary Ellen to greet any customers. She'd practiced saying *aloha* and *welcome* but now she couldn't remember the word for *welcome*. It would not be appropriate, anyway.

This was not a dream like she'd had after seeing his photo and awakening the next morning trying to get her breath.

In front of her stood the man whose photo had made its way to San Francisco. The photo that had changed her routine existence, like an hourglass being turned upside down, and started life anew.

Now, however, the sand in the hourglass seemed to have filtered down to her feet.

He was not a black-and-white photo. Thick hair, slightly mussed, perhaps by the trade winds, looked black. But not his eyes. They were deep blue and seemed to be staring as though questioning her heart and mind and soul. He would find nothing there, for she felt depleted. His handsome, bronzed face held a more rugged appearance than in the photo. His full, creamy brown lips reminded her of the coffee she'd had at the restaurant, and she could almost taste the delicious flavor. She moistened her dry lips with the tip of her tongue.

This was her Mr. C.

No. Not hers.

An arch of one dark eyebrow appeared to be a command for her to speak.

"Breanna." Her voice was shaky. "Is she. . .with you?"

His nostrils flared, and a firmness settled on his lips. "I do not know a Breanna." He folded his muscular arms across his broad chest that was covered by a multi-colored, short-sleeved shirt, open at the neck. His stance widened with the movement of his right foot, and he shifted his weight. "Tell me your story about this. . .Breanna. The tale you apparently told Rose. And others, it seems."

His jaw tightened. She sensed he was holding back anger.

"Breanna is my sister," she said, surprised that her voice had strengthened. But the matter of Breanna took precedence over anything else. While he stared at her intently, she told him about the photo and the exchange of letters.

"You read the letters?"

She had to admit that she had only seen the envelopes. "But through the letters, it was arranged that she would come here and meet you. A Mr. C. Honeycutt."

Instead of denying or admitting anything, he gave a short laugh. "I suspect you have a vivid imagination about all this."

"Are you C. Honeycutt?"

Moving one arm to his waist, he made a gallant bow. "Clay-bourne Honeycutt, at your service, ma'am." He straightened and raised an eyebrow again. "And who might you be?"

"Mar—" She stopped and closed her eyes. He seemed to think this was some kind of joke. "I am the sister of Breanna Colson, who came here to meet you." Mary Ellen lifted her chin and gazed at him. Good looks could certainly mask a scoundrel, and she suspected that's exactly what he was.

His lowering those long dark lashes over his eyes for a moment infuriated her. She pointed to the white dress on the dress form. "I have been making this for Breanna's marriage to you. Now, you can tell me what you know about this, or

I can contact the authorities."

His focus seemed to be on the wedding dress, and he appeared thoughtful for a moment. Then his deep blue gaze fell upon her again. "What about this scenario?" His head lowered just a bit, and his eyes seemed to dance. "Maybe you don't have a sister. Maybe you made this up, having seen my name on papers passing through the office on the mainland."

Her jaw developed a mind of its own, and she didn't seem able to close her mouth. His audacity rendered her speechless.

"Maybe you have been influenced by this picture-bride activity and decided to become one yourself." He gestured toward the wedding dress. "You say you were reluctant for your sister to come to Hawaii. But you're making a wedding dress for her?" He scoffed. "Your stories don't add up. Hold it. Don't move."

Moving had not been an option since he walked through the door. But that sounded like a threat, and she was now about to bolt. Just then, the spark that had been in his photo appeared in his eyes. What was it? Daring? Skepticism? Challenge? He grinned. "I can picture you in that dress. Looks like it's just your size. I propose that the dress is yours, and it is you, not some"—he spread his hands for emphasis—"some illusive sister, who wishes to marry."

"Why. . .why would I want to marry you?" she managed to say above the thundering of her heart.

He shrugged. "I wouldn't know. I certainly wouldn't want to marry someone like me."

Mary Ellen had never experienced anything like she was feeling. The world seemed to have stopped turning—or at least in her mind. Time was suspended. She could not look away from the eyes that challenged her. It was as if she was feeling what she had felt before Breanna snatched his photo and that ridiculous possibility from her. Here that photo-man stood in front of her, saying the dress was for her, that she wanted to marry, and he even used the word *propose*.

Where had her senses gone? Mentally, emotionally, and maybe even physically, she was still at sea. Her world had been shaken when her parents died. But she had known what to do. She'd had to be strong for Breanna. She had to have an emotionally controlled life to set the right example. But now, she felt like an earthquake had happened inside her, and she knew not where to turn.

Along with the wreckage, however, was a tiny flame. Somewhere deep inside, she was able to think. "I saw your photo. I saw the name *C. Honeycutt*, the note saying your occupation was with a sugar plantation and you wanted an American wife. The address was on the photo."

Feeling like she might topple over, she put one foot in front of another and made her way to the counter. She sat on the high stool in front of the cash register.

That didn't help much. He turned to face her. "You say you look like your sister?"

How many times must she continue to remind herself and everyone else that she was plain compared to Breanna? "She is five years younger, more outgoing, prettier." She glared at him. "And much more trusting."

He kept staring. She refused to look away no matter how piercing, dark, and probing his eyes. Finally, he spoke in a low, serious tone. "I can imagine many young women being more trusting." He shook his head briefly. "But I'm trying to imagine a young woman being prettier than you."

That remark stung because she felt he was making fun of her. Something inside her seemed to burst. Maybe like things exploding during the earthquake that caused the fires back in San Francisco.

She closed her eyes against the pictures that flooded her mind, like a group of photos laid out on a tabletop for others to view. The first was when she was seven and Breanna was two. Mary Ellen had been so proud of having lost her two front teeth, knowing big-girl teeth would come in. But a friend of her mother talked about Breanna's getting her teeth while Mary Ellen lost hers. Before that, everyone commented on how beautiful the baby was. Mary Ellen had thought so, too, and it was fine with her. But when the comment was made about teeth, Mary Ellen felt ugly, no longer proud of growing up, and learned to smile with her mouth closed.

Then Mary Ellen had to look and act like a proper young lady, while Breanna was always the baby, the last child their mother could have, and Mary Ellen was supposed to set the right example.

She couldn't say these things to Mr. C. And she could not comment on the pretty remark as if she believed a word of it. But maybe he didn't mean Mary Ellen was pretty. Maybe he really was trying to imagine how Breanna could be pretty while he looked at Mary Ellen.

While the presence and words of Mr. C. had so knocked Mary Ellen off her equilibrium, she could imagine that Breanna would have been completely swept off her feet. Not that she thought he had any charm. Yet she could imagine that he might. But then, she was still influenced by the photo. This. . .this Mr. C. could very well be a vile scoundrel, and he was definitely arrogant.

"Have I rendered you speechless, Mar. . .?"

Mar? Then she realized she hadn't told him her name. "Miss Colson," she said formally. "And no. I have plenty of speech. I'm just trying to figure out where to start. Until I have proof you did not send that photo, I cannot trust you. That would be the ultimate foolishness."

"I see." He gazed at the ceiling. "I suppose I must prove my innocence to you." He exhaled heavily. "You said there was an address on the photo."

"General delivery. Hilo Post Office."

"Let's go."

She stammered, looking around. "I have. . .we have customers that could—" He interrupted. "This shop operated before you came here. I think it can continue. Now, if you're telling the truth, let's go to the post office."

Those challenging eyes. What did he have in mind? Abduct her for illegal reasons? But if so, then maybe she would end up with her sister. "Just a moment." She went in back to tell the women at the sewing machines she had to leave.

"Aila, will you tell Pilar I'll be back soon? I need to go somewhere with Mr. Honeycutt."

"Oooh." Aila's response sounded like a song, and her eyes twinkled. "Anybody would go with Mr. Clay. You go on. He could charm the coffee bean off the Kona bush."

Mary Ellen wasn't sure she should risk her reputation by being seen with him. But for the possibility of finding out something about Breanna, she had no choice. "This is strictly business," she said staunchly.

The woman's eyebrows traveled up. "His business is making sugar." Aila giggled. Mary Ellen stared at her, and the woman ducked her head and returned to her table and the sewing machine.

Mary Ellen stood until the machine began to whirr. She reached over to a table and picked up small scissors, which she slipped into her skirt pocket.

"I'm ready," she said, returning to the front room. Her quick step halted when she felt something beneath her shoe and heard the faint crunch of a little seed pearl being crushed.

❧

"Shall we walk or ride?" Claybourne Honeycutt asked.

Matilda had mentioned seeing his car and had said there were only three in Hilo, other than rentals. The white vehicle parked down the street a couple of buildings away must be his. Why had he not parked in front of the dress shop? Had he walked up there and stood outside, observing her?

Her glance at him revealed that daring look in his eyes and slight upward turn of his lips. "How far is it?"

"Within looking distance. See the ocean down there?"

She gazed toward the wharf and saw a steamer anchored

in Hilo Bay. Tall palm trees swayed gracefully against a clear blue sky. "The post office is in the ocean?"

"I deserved that," he said. "Actually, the post office is located on the corner of Kamehameha and Waianuenue."

Those syllables rolled off his tongue as smoothly as the gentle waves caressing the seashore.

"Incidentally," he said, "across from the post office is the depot of the Hawaii Consolidated Railway. Our sugarcane is transported by rail from the fields to the mill and on down here for shipping."

Mary Ellen thought she would like to know more about this sugar business but pretended disinterest in case he still thought she had traveled over two thousand miles just to meet him.

She wouldn't have.

Would she?

But. . .Breanna had.

She felt her skirt brush against her legs, caused by her brisk pace and the warm breeze.

Many people were on the sidewalks, some coming out of shops and others going in. A couple of young women in Western dress stood across the street. "Aloha, Clay."

He returned the greeting. They seemed to smile at her before entering the restaurant. A man on a horse rode up the street. He was wearing a cowboy hat with flowers around the band. He tipped the brim with his fingers. "Aloha, Mr. Clay. Miss."

Clay laughed lightly when she turned to look after the man as he rode past. "The flowers?" he said. "People who are not from Hawaii question that. It's a common practice for paniolos to wear a band of flowers on their hats."

"Paniolos?"

"Cowboys. Matilda, whom I understand you met, is from Texas, and she still calls the paniolos cowboys."

"Do they mind?"

He shook his head. "There's a mixture of peoples and

languages and cultures here. We tend to accept the differences and don't get upset about them."

"So I've noticed. Not even about a young girl who—"

He stopped and faced her. "Of course I care if you have a missing sister. And I also care about being falsely accused. The sooner we get this cleared up, the better." He strode faster down the sidewalk.

She kept pace with him. She would run if necessary.

He reached the door of the building before she did and held it open for her to enter. A postal clerk stepped up to the opening. "Aloha."

"Jennings," Clay said, "do you have any general delivery mail for me?"

"You picked up your mail this morning, Clay."

"I'm aware of that." Clay laughed lightly. "This would be addressed only to C. Honeycutt in general delivery."

"I'll check."

Clay's smug glance seemed to say that was proof he hadn't received general delivery mail.

The man returned holding several letters. "Here you are. C. Honeycutt. I didn't know about the box. Sorry." He spread his hands and chuckled. "But what do I know? I'm only the postmaster." He handed the letters over. "Looks like you haven't picked them up in a while."

Mr. C. Honeycutt's bronzed coloring seemed to fade. Mary Ellen tried to give him a smug look, but he kept staring at the letters. Finally, he thanked Jennings and hastened to the door.

As soon as they stepped outside, she reached to jerk the letters from his hand.

He held them away, looking at them.

"This is proof that you received mail through general delivery."

He handed her the envelopes. "This is proof, all right. But not about me."

Mary Ellen shuffled through them. There were three. All

addressed to Breanna Colson, c/o Mr. C. Honeycutt. The return address was Mary Ellen Colson, San Francisco, California.

"She. . .she didn't get my letters. She didn't know I was coming."

"That explains why she didn't meet you or send word." Clay smiled broadly, and his dark eyes danced with a gleam in them.

"I realize that. But. . ." Mary Ellen felt the fear that sounded in her voice. "Where is my sister? Why did she not write to me? Why do you say you know nothing about this? Something isn't right. I have to go to the police."

જ

When she jerked away from his outstretched hand, Clay dropped it to his side. She did not trust him. And the fear in her eyes and voice was real.

He hated seeing the pain on her face. This young woman was beginning to believe the worst. She had paled considerably.

"Look. This involves me and the name of Honeycutt, too. I know this may sound selfish to you, but I know what the newspapers can do to a business if there's a scandal. And with your story, the implication is against me. I have a right to clear my name. Can you agree?"

She drew in a deep breath and weighed her words carefully. "Your name was on your photo, and someone had a box at the post office in your name."

"No," he said quickly. "Anyone could send mail to anyone's name. Now, do you have the photo?"

"My sister has it."

"But you saw it?"

"Yes, Breanna and I saw it at the same time. She was intrigued immediately."

She *was intrigued*? He could return to that thought later. Now, he needed to concentrate on her sister and the consequences of a police investigation. "Okay. Let's look at this realistically."

Despite the skepticism in her eyes, he continued. "The

name Honeycutt means something around here." She shook her head and frowned. "That's not pride. It's fact. The police would have a hard time believing I had anything to do with this. And all the evidence you have against me is letters you sent to a post office box."

"I have a missing sister. And I can prove it."

Now that was a problem.

"Let's go back inside." She didn't pull away when he took her arm and led her in. He went again to the postmaster. "Jennings, I think somebody took a box in my name and got mail in my name. Maybe someone from my office. Can you check around and see if anyone remembers my making those arrangements?"

Clay stood silently beside Mary Ellen while the man checked.

Jennings returned. "Nobody remembers it. We get a lot of mail for you, but not through general delivery. Sorry if something went wrong. But you know we have hundreds of visitors who get their mail general delivery. We put the person's name on a card that says HOLD TILL ASKED FOR and put them in those alphabetical boxes. It's not something we try to remember."

"Okay. Tell me this. Who picks up my mail?"

The man looked as though he had lost his mind. "Um, you. Your employees. Your secretary, someone from your office. Are you looking for something in particular?"

"No. It's fine. Thanks, Jennings. But ask your workers to give more thought about who asked for a general delivery box in my name."

Mary Ellen headed for the door before him this time. She paused on the sidewalk, her eyes brimming with determination as if they were screaming for the police. Maybe he could reassure her. "The police would do more than I've done. They would question if anyone in the post office noticed anything unusual."

"So you want me to trust you instead of the police? Is that

what any intelligent, sensible person would do?"

"Yes, because I have a better chance of getting to the bottom of this than the police."

"How?"

"I can ask questions without anyone being afraid they're going to be arrested. You heard Jennings say that only about six people can get my mail. I'll get the truth out of them."

"But you told me anyone can get a post office box in your name."

"But not just anyone could have had my photo."

He thought he had her there. But she came back with, "You're the suspect."

"But I'm not the person guilty of anything. Just give me a chance."

Her blue eyes flashed. "So, begin the investigation, and I'll let you know how well you're doing."

He had to think fast. "Let's go to the immigration office."

"Matilda, Rose, and I have done that."

"But I haven't." He turned and strode down the sidewalk. She couldn't very well physically detain him. He tried to hide the grin he felt forming on his lips when he heard the fast tapping of those pointed-toe shoes as she hurried to catch up with him.

Miss Colson was giving him a chance to prove himself and help find her sister. A chance. But she had seen his photo along with her sister. The sister had been interested—but this Miss Colson had not been.

He'd never had to work at gaining a woman's interest.

Herein was a challenge.

Different. Even intriguing.

After they would get through this sister problem, perhaps he'd work on the one who had not been interested in him. After all, she was quite an attractive blond. Had spirit, too.

He slowed when she reached him. "Tell me again exactly what was on the back of that photo."

She repeated what he'd already heard several times. "I've

told you everything. No. Something else. You said you were a moral person. That seemed like a good thing at the time. Now, I wonder if you. . .someone was trying to convince us of that because he had ulterior motives."

Clay's mind stuck on the word *moral.*

"I'd never say that." When she gave him a quick look, he amended the statement. "I mean, of course I am. But one doesn't go around saying it."

She looked doubtful.

Who would say that?

He knew. The game.

The question he had asked Mak returned to his mind. *What would a man want with an eighteen-year-old girl?* Mak's glance had meant, plain as day, it depends on the man. Clay shuddered inwardly at the myriad of answers.

Maybe he should let the police handle this. Otherwise, she might discover that Mr. C. Honeycutt is—although indirectly—involved.

❧

Mr. C. had said one thing that made sense. If Mary Ellen went to the police, he might be jailed and then not be in any position to help her.

And, too, Breanna did not get Mary Ellen's letters. She didn't know her sister was coming to Hawaii. But why did no one know about Breanna? Or was everyone simply claiming not to know?

"She expected to meet you, Mr. C. If no one showed up to meet her, she would have tried to get in touch with you. Someone met her."

"We'll check it all out."

When they arrived at the immigration office, Akemi greeted them with her beautiful, sweet smile, her black eyes filled with warmth and welcome. "You found your Mr. C. Aloha, Mr. Clay." She made her little bow, and Mary Ellen thought her adorable.

Akemi summoned Mr. Hammeur. He entered the room,

smiling, but one glance at Mary Ellen, and he exhibited the same aloofness she'd detected earlier.

Clay asked Mr. Hammeur if he'd checked the passenger list and if Miss Breanna Colson had disembarked.

"Yes, of course. The captain presented his passenger list to me. He assured me that all passengers for this island had disembarked."

"Do you remember the night she was to arrive?"

Mr. Hammeur's responses were what they had been earlier.

Clay thanked Mr. Hammeur, who then left the front room. Mary Ellen watched as Mr. C. walked over to Akemi, who was folding letters and putting them into envelopes. She did not look up.

"Akemi," Mr. C. said softly. "You know my photo had to go out from here. The Japanese man's official form was sent to the mainland. How could that have happened?"

"I do not know."

"Did some Japanese man come in? Did you do him a favor? Or perhaps the wife of a Japanese man?"

"No Japanese man could come in without a boss, like you. It is not allowed. I would be deported for that."

"A restaurant owner might. Someone who doesn't work on the plantation."

"No. If anyone needed me to help with a letter or a form, I wouldn't do it from here."

Mary Ellen believed her. She felt that Mr. C., although asking kindly, was torturing the poor girl.

"Is there any way my photo could have gone out from this office? Has anyone ever helped you with the mail?"

Akemi's lower lip trembled. "Please, Mr. Clay. Don't ask me any more."

He lifted a hand, as if to say *wait*. He left the room. Soon he returned. "I told Mr. Hammeur that you're not feeling well and need some air. Please, Akemi. Come outside with us."

She did.

They walked down the sidewalk to a bench. Mary Ellen sat beside Akemi.

Mr. C. stood in front of her. "Who has helped you?"

"Only Geoffrey. He's not like his brother, but he's good. He wouldn't hurt anyone. I know he would not."

Mary Ellen watched Clay look at the sky and call on the Almighty and then glance at her. "That, Miss Colson, was a prayer."

"He would come and talk to me when Mr. Hammeur went to lunch. It was during a time when a big shipment of men were to come in. I was busy. He took mail to the post office a few times. He sealed some envelopes for me. I saw no harm in it."

"It's all right. He takes my mail to the post office all the time. And we don't know if he tampered with your mail. You didn't do anything wrong, Akemi."

"Mr. Hammeur will think so."

"Maybe we can get this straightened out without Mr. Hammeur."

Mr. C. obviously knew more than he was saying. Before Mary Ellen could ask who Geoffrey was, they were assaulted with the *chahoooga, chahoooga!*

Matilda parked in front of them, jumped out of her car, and waved an envelope. "You have a letter from San Francisco, Mary Ellen. It was just delivered to the Matti-Rose."

Mary Ellen reached into her skirt pocket and took out the scissors. She opened them and used an edge to slice open the envelope. A quick glance around revealed curious looks from Akemi and Matilda. Clay's mouth opened slightly, and his eyes turned toward heaven. If he thought she'd put those scissors in her pocket as a weapon to use against him if necessary, he was right.

Another envelope was inside the one she opened, addressed to Mary Ellen Colson, c/o Uncle Harv. "It's Breanna's handwriting," she said. "See how she curls her letters?"

She read Breanna's first:

Dearest Mary Ellen,

Everything is going so well for me. I'm on the island of Oahu. Will write more when I have time. I have so much to tell you.

Don't worry about me, but write and let me know how things are with you and how that wedding dress is coming along. You must come here.

Love,
Breanna

"What's the address?" Clay asked.

Mary Ellen let out a sharp breath. "Breanna Colson. General delivery. Post office, Oahu, Hawaii."

"Oh, we can find her then," Matilda said. "She's all right."

"I'll find her." Clay said. "Someone used my photo and my name. I will find out who."

"Her safety is the most important thing at the moment, Mr. C. Whoever is behind this is secondary."

His bronzed skin deepened in color. "That goes without saying."

"Is that another letter there, dear?" Matilda said.

"Oh." Mary Ellen unfolded the sheet of San Francisco immigration office stationery. "This is from Uncle Harv":

My dear Mary Ellen,

This letter came to you from Breanna. She obviously sent this after you left for Hawaii. I'm sure you two are having a wonderful time. I hope you are well and find time to write to me.

Affectionately,
Your Uncle Harv

Akemi's voice was full of hope. "Your sister is okay now. She say she okay."

"Yes, but why is she in Oahu? She came here to meet Mr. C." Mary Ellen had thought of him so long as Mr. C., she couldn't easily think of him as Clay. "I don't understand this. She didn't mention Mr. C. in her letter, but she was so looking forward to meeting him." She glanced from Akemi to Matilda. "She must be devastated that she wasn't met." She took a deep breath. "If that's the case."

"I will telegraph Oahu," Clay said.

"Telegraph the post office?" Mary Ellen saw that Matilda and Akemi were looking at him with the same kind of questioning she felt.

"I have business friends and relatives in Oahu. I will telegraph them, and you will get your information." He paused. "Now. I will go now."

"Do that." Mary Ellen knew her voice sounded short instead of grateful. But this Mr. C. Honeycutt was one strange bird. She could only pray that Breanna was safe. For now, she would pretend she trusted him.

What choice did she have?

Choice?

Of course she had a choice. She deposited the scissors into her pocket, lifted her chin, and said, "Let's go."

"And I will chaperone," Matilda said with a lilt in her voice. Her green eyes sparkled.

"Protect me might be a better word," Clay said, "since Miss Colson carries a weapon in her pocket."

"Oh, Pilar had gone to get us sandwiches when I left. I asked Aila to tell her I would be back soon."

"Did you tell her you were leaving with Clay?"

Mary Ellen felt uneasy, remembering how the worker had acted. "Yes, I did."

"Then Pilar will understand if you don't hurry back. Nevertheless, Akemi," Matilda said, "would you run across the street and let someone know Mary Ellen won't be back for a while?"

"Sure thing, okay." Akemi lifted her graceful hand as she turned to go.

"I'll use the telegraph system at my dock office," Clay said.

Mary Ellen was grateful to Matilda for her thoughtfulness or curiosity, whichever it was, in accompanying them. She was not comfortable being alone with the enigmatic Mr. C., who aroused a myriad of fluctuating emotions in her.

nine

Mary Ellen watched Clay handle the telegraph system. Matilda explained, "They get orders from all over the world, since the U.S. annexation. Sugar is Hawaii's biggest business, you know."

She'd heard that, but it wasn't what mattered at the moment. She was torn between thinking Mr. C. might find Breanna and the question of how he knew where and whom to call.

He said the words as he punched out the code. "Seeking whereabouts of Breanna Colson. Eighteen years old. Blond. Blue eyes." He glanced at Mary Ellen and back at the machine. "Pretty. Contact sugar mill at the dock on Hawaii. Have Geoffrey contact me ASAP."

"Do you think he's wiring the Oahu Post Office?"

Matilda shook her head. "No. That would be his brother, Thomas. The Honeycutts own plantations and sugar mills in Oahu, too. Clay has access to many contacts." She smiled. "Don't you think, Mary Ellen, this is just miscommunication between you and your sister?"

"Not entirely. Our letters not getting to each other is one thing. But her not mentioning the man she came to meet tells me something is not right."

"But her letter did not sound as if she were in trouble, did it?"

Mary Ellen took the letter from her pocket and read it again. "No. She sounds like she's looking forward to a wedding. But right here is the Mr. C. in the photo. Is there someone who looks like him?"

Matilda sighed. "Ahh. Nobody looks like your Mr. C. He is like the racehorse my Jane rode that beat the king's horse in the royal race. Some animals are simply one of a kind."

At Mary Ellen's quick glance, Matilda added, "And some people."

"Well," Mary Ellen said, "there are two sides to people. The outside and the inside."

"So true. I think you should get to know your Mr. C.'s insides."

She suspected that would be much too complicated.

He came over to them. "The word is out. The communication system isn't always efficient, but the sugar office in Oahu will get the message and pass along the information. All Oahu will be looking for Miss Breanna. I will be contacted as soon as a reply comes in."

"I keep hearing the name Geoffrey."

Clay nodded. "He's one of my and my brother's employees who may be able to help us."

❧

Clay knew he wouldn't be able to keep his mind on the account ledgers, so he needn't go to the sugar mill, or to the other five appointments that had been on his agenda for the day.

Everything pointed to Geoffrey. If he was involved in this, Breanna would likely be safe. If not, there were questions Clay himself couldn't answer. And he didn't want to accuse Geoffrey before he had some facts.

Clay felt useless until later in the day when one of his employees called to him. "Wire for you from the Oahu office."

He read the message hurriedly: "BREANNA WITH ME. ALL FINE. GEOFFREY."

As fast as the system would work, Clay punched out the code that Breanna's sister was in Hawaii and worried. He demanded that Geoffrey have the girl wire her sister within thirty minutes.

Geoffrey opted for an hour.

Clay agreed, feeling both anger and relief. But the anger wasn't directed only at Geoffrey. The scripture he'd learned when a child at the mission school circled around in his brain—*"Be sure your sin will find you out."* On second thought, it was beginning to look like neither he nor Geoffrey had a brain, maybe just empty space.

A short while later, Clay stood outside the Matti-Rose Hawaiian and Western Wear Shop, watching Miss Colson, as he had done that morning. Amazing, what a few hours could do to a person's thinking.

Earlier, he had seen her as a lovely blond, but also as one who had invented an elaborate ruse to get to him. She had even been getting her wedding dress ready. Thinking about that, he realized how uncouth and arrogant he'd been that morning. His dad would not have been proud of him.

Now, he stood looking, not at someone with whom he might play games, but a young woman who had traveled many miles to find her younger sister. And she was making a wedding dress for that same sister.

As if sensing him there, Miss Colson's head slowly turned. She looked over her shoulder, and their gazes held. After a moment of showing no emotion, she again turned her attention to the dress. He felt that indicated she didn't expect anything from him—not anything good anyway.

He looked around, as if seeing the main street of Hilo in a new way. Maybe he was seeing himself. And that, too, was based on selfishness. For as long as he could remember, he'd been occupied with how he saw women. Right now, he was concerned with how this woman saw him.

&

When Mary Ellen looked around at Mr. C., she thought of what Mrs. Dampers had said many times. Whenever an orphan claimed she would do something like study harder, scrub better, or clean her plate, Mrs. Dampers would thrust her big fists into her ample sides, scowl, and say, "Missie, that's only lip service. The proof of the pudding is in the eating."

Mary Ellen took her words to mean a person's word meant little without the action. Come to think of it, the Bible had something to say about that: *"Faith without works is dead."*

That wasn't exactly the same thing, but she felt it also meant lip service without action didn't mean much.

Since she didn't know what to think of the enigmatic Mr. C., she had to rely on proverbs and sayings and clichés. Right now, a dominant one was *handsome is as handsome does*. So far, he was lacking in the *does*. Although he appeared to be helping, he also seemed to be holding back information.

She did not turn when the bell tinkled.

Mr. C. and Pilar spoke to each other like familiar friends. "I told Mary Ellen," Pilar said, "that you know everyone in Oahu and you will find her sister."

"I do have some news. Mar—"

She felt her shoulders rise. He must have noticed for he quickly said, "Miss Colson, a friend and employee of mine knows your sister. He is to have her wire my office in less than an hour."

Mary Ellen had let him talk to her back. Now, words seemed to fail her. Those ambivalent feelings. Was Breanna really all right? Or was Mr. C. pretending to help when, in reality, he was involved in Breanna's disappearance? If Breanna wired from Oahu, would there be a request for a ransom?

Mary Ellen turned. She could only shake her head. "I don't know you, Mr. Honeycutt. I need someone to accompany us. Matilda will return soon."

Pilar laughed, and he scowled. Then she cleared her throat and appeared quite somber.

Mr. C. spread his hands. "There's a building full of people. Dockworkers are all around. People on the street. Why, all of a sudden—"

"Why? Because you've led me on too many wild goose chases, Mr. C. I am tired of that. I go to your office, and there's no telegram from my sister, and then what? And how can I know it's from her? You might have me on another wild-goose chase."

His brows almost met. "You have goose chases on the mainland?"

"This is not about gooses." She closed her eyes and breathed in through her nose. "I mean, geese. And I will not be duped. Do you understand *duped*?"

Further comments were cut off by *chaooooga, chaooooga*.

Pilar's smile and the lifting of Mr. C.'s eyes toward the ceiling indicated they knew who should accompany them to the sugar office.

❧

Inside the office, Clay stood back where neither Miss Colson nor Matilda would be looking straight at him, lest his concern be reflected in his face. He turned away from his desk and looked out the window away from the dock. The white sand beach stretched out between the softly lapping ocean on one side and palm-fringed trees on the other. This should be a day for walking along that path with a beautiful woman instead of having one standing in his office, her every expression one of distrust, suspicion, and dislike.

But that was the way of it and—

"Your wire is coming from Oahu, sir," an office worker announced.

Clay read it as it came in:

MARY ELLEN. WHAT A SURPRISE. CAN'T WAIT TO SEE YOU. WILL ARRIVE MONDAY. WILL WIRE TIME. LOVE, BREANNA.

"See," Clay said. "All that worry for nothing. Your sister is fine. It's just that you two communicate about as well as our interisland system, which is almost nil."

"Communication between me and my sister is not the problem, Mr. C. If this is on the level, then it's a problem between you and your"—she paused—"your *friend*."

How well he knew. But he wasn't going to admit it until he had to.

"Send a wire to her," she said. "Ask if she's alone and where she is."

He did. The words came back:

WITH GEOFFREY'S PARENTS. HE AND I ARE IN LOVE.

"Geoffrey?" she said, shaking her head and looking helpless. Her eyes closed as tears trickled down her cheeks.

How many times had he said he had never hurt any woman. He could no longer claim that. This one was hurting. "You want to send another message?"

"Just tell her I love her and be sure to telegram what time she will arrive."

She turned to Matilda. "Breanna says she's all right and in love with someone named Geoffrey," repeating the message as if Matilda hadn't heard it and Mary Ellen couldn't believe it.

"Then she is all right," Clay said.

"According to the telegram, yes. But I can't be sure." Her eyes threatened him. "She came to Hawaii because she was in love with you."

He scoffed and heard his voice rise at least an octave. "In love with a photo?"

Her lips trembled. Her eyes became teary again, and she turned away. Matilda put her arm around Miss Colson's shoulders.

ॐ

Clay dressed in his finest, taking particular care to look like a decent, respectable gentleman attending church. Before the service, he spoke to Jacob.

"Sorry I couldn't bring Geoffrey with me, Jacob. But I talked to him, and he may be here on Monday. I'll let him know you'd like to see him."

Disappointment settled on Jacob's face but he thanked Clay and turned to shake another person's hand and speak to him.

"Good morning, Clay." That was Rose's voice. He turned to see her, Matilda, and Miss Colson. The older women, as usual, were dressed like owners of a dress shop, in latest Western fashion.

Miss Colson looked serene but lovely, as if everything about her was perfect, exactly as it should be. Any decent, respectable gentleman would be proud to win her approval.

Miss Colson did not extend her hand; she simply nodded as an acknowledgment that he existed.

He felt his pasted-on smile disappear when Matilda spoke in a reprimanding way. "Well, Claybourne Honeycutt. It's about time you got yourself back in church."

Leave it to Matilda!

"Matilda, Rose." Jeannette Hammeur, holding her skirt with one hand and her hat with the other, rushed up to them. "Oh, Miss Colson. That's right, isn't it?"

At the affirmative nod, the woman frowned. "Did you find your sister?"

When Miss Colson said yes, Jeannette lifted her hands. "Praise the Lord. I prayed you would." She turned to Matilda and Rose. "Do you have any word on that dress I wanted?"

Clay took the opportunity to try to show there was a hospitable side to him. "Miss Colson, perhaps you'd be interested in the history of this church."

Her chin lifted, as did her eyes, cornflower blue today with a touch of indignation. Her gaze held his. "Perhaps," she said.

He took her elbow, felt the exquisite material of her dress and the warmth of her flesh beneath it. With an almost indiscernible movement, she shifted her arm away but continued to walk alongside him. He pointed to the top of the church.

"That steeple is one hundred-feet high."

She didn't say anything. He looked down at her upturned face. The pert little hat covered most of her blond hair. But a couple of locks that begged to be wrapped around a finger lay along the sides of her face. Her eyes were as blue as the summer sky, sparked by the silver glint of the sun. They turned to gaze into his. Her full lips, the color of coral, parted slightly.

"What's the significance of that?"

The significance? "Well, Miss Colson—" He quickly put his hand to his mouth and cleared his throat. He'd been about to tell her the significance was that she was quite lovely.

But her focus had returned to the steeple. He felt it coming from deep inside and couldn't hold it back. He laughed. "Sorry," he said. "That's as far as my history lesson goes about that steeple."

"I just wondered. Is there a bell in it?"

It began to ring. Ah, saved by the bell. "Complete with a young boy swinging on a rope. Now this might interest you. Matilda's brother, Reverend Russell, preached here for more than thirty years. He taught in the mission school and was greatly admired and respected."

Matilda and Rose caught up with them near the entrance. Miss Colson thanked him and joined the other two women, who walked down and sat in a pew on the left side of the church, a few rows from the front where Akemi sat. People near them began to turn and be introduced to Miss Colson.

Clay found a seat at the right on the second pew from the back, near the aisle. He surely failed the history lesson. He could have told Miss Colson about the ti plants that surrounded the church, planted at a time when many natives believed the plant warded off evil spirits, so they felt brave enough to enter the church. After being inside, they were presented with the gospel message.

While the choir sang, his gaze scanned the church, where he had attended most of his young life. He could have told her the church was made of lava rock, bonded together by crushed coral, sand, and oil from kukui nuts. She might like to know the king and queen had attended this church.

He should have said the current pastor was from the mainland and that the congregation liked his stories about America. Clay listened more closely when he began one of those stories.

"I came from the mountains of Colorado where there are a lot of snowy winters," the pastor said.

Hawaii didn't have snowfalls like in the U.S. and Europe, but Clay knew much about the snow on Mauna Kea, so he got the preacher's image in his mind. He prided himself on having been an unofficial tour guide for more than a few European and American young woman. He'd formed a few snowballs during a ski trip, and he'd experienced the enveloping of the cold snow when he'd taken a few tumbles down the slopes.

The congregation was exchanging glances and smiles as the pastor told of his personal mishaps on the slopes. Then he began to talk about thoughts being like a snowball.

He presented a vivid picture of a thought turning into contemplation, and from there into desire, and then action, and that little tiny snowball had rolled down a hill and become too big and too cold and too heavy to budge or melt. The preacher was talking about sin.

Clay became increasingly warm and uncomfortable despite the snow sermon. He'd simply wanted to go to the snowy mountain and pick up a snowball here and there. He wouldn't let them roll down the hill. Just hold them awhile.

And no, his snowballs hadn't rolled down the mountain. That was fun, exciting, a game. Yes, it had all started with a snowball of a thought.

It seemed to be slipping from his hand, threatening to roll down the hill.

Considering the uncertainty about Miss Colson's sister and Geoffrey, how long would he hold onto the snowball?

ॐ

After the church service ended, and Mary Ellen felt she'd been introduced to everyone, she turned to Akemi to compliment her on her beautiful kimono. By the time Akemi said, "Thank you," Clay Honeycutt was in the aisle, motioning to the man who had given the announcements and led the prayer.

When the man reached them, Clay introduced him as

Jacob Grant, a teacher and assistant to the pastor. Then Clay surprised her with his invitation. "If you ladies and Jacob don't have lunch plans, perhaps—"

Matilda turned to them. "I've already made reservations at the Japanese restaurant. You young people can have those. Or join us, either one."

"I'm sorry, Clay." Jacob said. "I do have other plans. Excuse me, please."

Mary Ellen wondered about the puzzled look on Clay's face and the furrowed brow of Jacob, as if he was truly sorry he couldn't join them. But it was presumptuous of Clay Honeycutt to assume she and Akemi might want to lunch with him. He might have asked sooner, unless this was a spur-of-the-moment impulsive idea.

Her glance at Akemi revealed the girl no longer smiled and her head was bowed. She was not looking at anyone. Was Mr. C. interested in Akemi?

Rose touched his arm. "Join us, Clay."

"No, I don't want to intrude."

"Intrude." Rose scoffed. "Clay, you're family."

Mary Ellen didn't know what to make of Rose having said Clay was family. On second thought, however, Matilda and Rose seemed to treat everyone like family.

"Some other time, perhaps. Good day, ladies."

Mary Ellen tried not to be obvious watching him being greeted by friendly people. Were they greeting him like that because they liked him, or were they welcoming him more like a prodigal son, as Matilda had intimated?

❧

At the restaurant after much discussion about food, Mary Ellen read from the menu. "I've never had this. So I'll try the fried calamari with saffron pepper sauce."

"Great choice," Matilda said. "And, remember, we can sample each other's food."

While they ate, Mary Ellen once again mentioned how much she admired Akemi's kimono.

"I am trying to show that I am proud to be Japanese. But since I have learned about God and Jesus, I cannot worship Buddha. Some do not understand that I can be Japanese and not worship Buddha. That is why I try to show them I care about the Japanese. Maybe even more now."

Mary Ellen saw the sadness on her face and was impressed that Akemi cared about the souls of her people. "Was it hard for you to leave your country?"

"Both sad and exciting," she said. "There is much poverty and disease in Japan. Most young men have come to Hawaii. Here they have job. Live in a beautiful place. Some bring picture bride so they have wife and children. That is better than most have in Japan."

"You must have been terribly disappointed when marriage didn't work out for you." Mary Ellen thought of Breanna. *What happened that she wasn't met by Mr. C.? Was she sad? Pretending all was well?*

"Yes, at first," Akemi said. "But now I think God had a different purpose for me. The plantation workers will not listen to haole talk about Jesus. But they listen to me. They feel sorry for me that I am not in their community and don't have a husband and children."

"We're your family, Akemi." Matilda patted the girl's arm.

Akemi smiled and nodded. "I know."

"Is that what you meant, Rose, when you told Mr. C. that he was your family?"

Rose's brow knitted. "Not exactly. His parents were killed in a shipwreck coming back from Scotland. That's when such a trip took months instead of days. There was a particularly bad storm. After that, Clay took over the business on this island, and it has thrived even more. He worked so hard. Now his brother and sister are settled in Oahu, and Clay runs this business like a shrewd businessman, in the best sense of the word."

Mary Ellen felt compassion for him, knowing the heartbreak of losing one's parents. Was she misjudging him?

But she had to remember: His photo had shown up in San Francisco. Breanna had corresponded with Mr. C. and come to Hawaii.

No. She mustn't ignore the signs that all was not right. She could not trust him completely, at least not until after she saw and talked with Breanna.

ten

After the wire came in with the boat's arrival time from Oahu, Clay talked to Jacob and told him all about it.

After a long, stone-faced silence, Jacob said, "I'll have to do a lot of praying about this one."

Clay figured he'd do a lot more than pray. Increased anger rose in him as the boat approached the harbor. Anger that Geoffrey had done this to him. Anger that Miss Colson had every right to press charges against Geoffrey for tampering with U.S. mail. Would anyone believe that Clay had not been involved? He could only hope that the younger sister had not been coerced in any way. But she had been. With Clay's photo.

What had Geoffrey been thinking?

He closed his eyes against the question that Mak had asked and feared the answer. The snowball sermon came to mind. He had a feeling God was telling him something.

And Geoffrey needed to be taught a lesson.

But so did Claybourne Honeycutt. He sensed more lessons were to come. This was not over; perhaps it was just beginning.

Clay stood apart from Mary Ellen, Rose, Matilda, and Akemi. He had a few choice questions for Geoffrey, and he didn't need anyone in the way when he got his answers. He could almost see the newspaper headlines about Claybourne Honeycutt being mixed up in a scandal of illegal and immoral activity. Breanna Colson only had to say one negative word, and both he and Geoffrey could be carted off to jail.

He recalled the anger he'd felt when one of his workers had deceived Akemi. How much worse for this to happen to a member of one's family. He shuddered to think if his sister had been eighteen and lured anywhere under false pretenses.

There they were. Geoffrey holding onto the arm of a young girl who did indeed resemble Mary Ellen. This one was all smiles. She was quite well-dressed. Her hair fell loose over her shoulders, and she held onto her wide-brimmed hat.

Geoffrey and the girl were laughing and talking and thanking the greeters who placed leis around their necks. They looked like a couple of youngsters playing—

Clay's thoughts stopped. That's exactly what Geoffrey was doing. Playing a game. And Claybourne Honeycutt was the one who had taught him.

A squeal of delight came from Mary Ellen as she rushed toward her sister. Breanna threw out her arms and ran. They shared a lengthy embrace until Mary Ellen stepped back and laid her hands on Breanna's shoulders. Her hand came up, and she caressed her younger sister's face.

Clay saw the resemblance and the differences. The young sister was quite pretty and seemed to exude a lively spirit. Mary Ellen was a few inches taller than her sister, who was a few pounds heavier. Breanna had a childlike quality about her that was appealing. He could readily see why Geoffrey would be enamored of her, as exhibited by his watching her every move.

But Mary Ellen was a lovely young woman who was trying to be an authority figure for her sister. He knew the feeling of taking authority, although his efforts had been in business rather than with his older siblings.

Geoffrey ambled up to them, all smiles, and from the corner of his eye, Clay saw Akemi walking toward them.

Clay took a deep breath. He did not return Geoffrey's wide smile. "You sent my photo to the mainland?"

"Yeah, but—"

"When you pretended to help Akemi?"

He scowled and looked toward Akemi. "I did help. But yeah—"

"You lured this—"

"I didn't lure—"

"You know this is illegal?"

"No." Geoffrey grimaced. "I never thought of that."

"You know it's immoral."

Geoffrey seemed to be comprehending. He began to shake his head. Dread filled his eyes.

Clay nodded and drew back his arm.

Someone grabbed his arm before his fist could hit its intended target. He turned his head quickly to identify who. Jacob?

"He's my brother."

Clay stared at him. Jacob held on until Clay relaxed his fist. "Your brother has acted totally irresponsibly. It also involves the Honeycutt reputation and yours, too, for that matter."

"I know," Jacob said. He faced his brother. "And this could mean Akemi loses her job."

Geoffrey scoffed and spread his hands. "That won't happen." He started to smile. In a flash, he landed on his backside, his mouth open, his fingers moving to his jaw and his eyes wide, his brown curls spilling over his forehead into his eyes. Jacob's arm was outstretched, his fist still clenched. "Like I said, he's my brother." He looked at Clay again.

"But you don't hit as hard as I do."

"No, but I don't want him knocked out. I want him to feel the impact of my fist and of what he's done."

Geoffrey moved.

"You get up, and I'll do it again," Jacob threatened.

Geoffrey settled back.

"Oh. Oh. Oh." Young Breanna rushed to his side and knelt. She brushed aside his unruly curls. "Are you all right, Geoffy?"

"It hurts." He looked at her with that sick cow expression that Clay had vowed he would never have about a woman.

She leaned his head against her shoulder. She looked up at Jacob. "You awful, awful man."

"I'm his older brother." His voice held authority. "And if he doesn't have enough sense to behave properly, it's time he got some knocked into him. I do believe in being my brother's keeper."

"He hasn't done anything wrong." She looked lovingly at Geoffrey, who basked in her attempted vindication of him. "He's good, and he's wonderful."

Matilda walked up. "I was thinking back, Geoffrey. How did you manage to get the photo in the envelope without being seen?"

He admitted what she appeared to have already surmised. He had gone to the bathroom at the inn to slip the photo inside the envelope.

"Stand back, dear." Breanna wasted no time in obeying. Matilda removed the lei from around Geoffrey's neck. She slammed it back and forth across his head. He covered his face with his hands.

When she finally quit, he wailed, "That has shells in it."

Matilda huffed. "I was hoping for shark teeth."

Clay stepped back when Akemi came up to Jacob and looked at him with those dark, doelike eyes of hers. Her soft voice trembled. "It is my fault, too. I should not have let him help me."

Jacob eyed Geoffrey but spoke to Akemi. "Did you ask him to help?"

She bowed her head and looked at the ground. "No. But I didn't mind. I am sorry. Don't be angry. Please forgive me."

"Akemi."

Clay had never heard Jacob say anyone's name so softly. He watched as Akemi lifted her head and her eyes to Jacob. Her face was full of adoration.

"Helping is all right, Akemi." Jacob was looking at her. "It's his deception that's wrong." Abruptly, he turned from her, slid a glance past Clay, and focused on Geoffrey.

What was going on?

&

Mary Ellen didn't think a sock on the jaw or a lei lashing would do much for the situation where Breanna was concerned. She would, however, take the route that Jacob had taken. "I am your older sister, Breanna. Regardless of how you feel, I have a responsibility."

"You're not going to have him arrested, are you?" Breanna's face clouded.

Tears or pleading wouldn't change Mary Ellen's position. "I don't know all the facts. We need to talk."

"She can have the bedroom across from yours," Matilda said to Mary Ellen.

"Excuse me," Akemi said. "I'm expected at work. But if you need me—"

None of them seemed to think it necessary she go with them and chance losing her job.

"Just one question," Jacob said. "How did Geoffrey go about starting to help you at the office?"

Akemi looked puzzled at the question. After a moment, she met Jacob's gaze. "He was very kind. We would talk about how my Bible classes with you were going. And my English."

"Bible," Jacob repeated. Mary Ellen saw the clench of his jaw and his fist as if he might punch Geoffrey again.

Akemi seemed to have noticed and said quickly, "And you. He would talk about what a good man you are."

Jacob glared at Geoffrey again, but his words were addressed to Akemi. "I think it's fine that you go to work, Akemi. You will not lose your job. If Mr. Hammeur needs to get word of this, the blame will fall on the coercion of Geoffrey. Be assured of that."

Akemi whispered. "Forgive me."

Jacob's eyes closed for a moment, and he shook his head. "You did nothing wrong."

"I try," she said, "to be perfect."

"You are." Jacob spoke so quickly, the entire group seemed stunned. Akemi turned and hastened across the sand as swiftly as her small feet and kimono would allow. Looking at the group around her, Mary Ellen saw that Jacob stared at the sand. Jacob reached out to his brother. Geoffrey accepted

Jacob's hand and stood.

As soon as Mary Ellen and her sister were away from the men and could speak alone, she asked, "Has everything really been all right with you, Breanna?" Matilda and Rose, walking behind them on the sidewalk, might hear, but that was fine. She needed the support of those two women.

"Better than you can imagine. I am sorry you've worried." Breanna's blue eyes danced with the glint of the sunlight, and her smile melted Mary Ellen's heart. "But I'm so glad you're here. We can talk now, woman to woman."

Mary Ellen was afraid to ask what that meant.

As soon as they arrived at the house, Rose began brewing tea. Matilda took cups down.

The tea was ready by the time the three men entered the house. Mary Ellen assured Rose and Matilda she did want them sitting in on the conversation.

They gathered around the kitchen table. Jacob sat directly across from Geoffrey. "Perhaps we should have a prayer before we start this discussion," Jacob said. They bowed their heads, and Jacob offered a brief prayer for guidance and restraint. After the *Amen*, he took the lead. "Tell us why you did this, Geoffrey."

"Well. You all know the men outnumber the women here two to one. I've seen all the women. Whenever any visitors or new ones come, most of them fall for Clay. I decided to get one for myself before she had a chance to see him. Women are crazy about him and I get leftovers."

Clay scoffed. "But you sent *my* picture."

"To get her attention. And it worked. Then after we began to write to each other, I sent my own picture and told her the truth. If I'd sent my picture in the beginning, she might have thrown it in the trash."

"Oh no, Geoffrey. I fell in love with you the moment I saw your photo. Nobody is more. . ." Breanna looked around and grimaced. "Nobody is more adorable than you. You are the cutest, most best-looking man I've ever seen."

His smile widened, matching hers, and their eyes seemed only for each other.

Finally, Breanna looked at Mary Ellen. "He sings. He plays the ukulele. And you should see him on a surfboard. He's wonderful."

Mary Ellen lifted a hand. "I understand. But you came here because you fell in love with the photo of Mr. C."

"Well." She shifted in her chair and pushed back a lock of hair. "Mr. C.'s photo did intrigue me. I mean, enough that I would have traveled this far just to see him. And I was going to take the immigration office job. I was going to make sure Mr. C. was as good as he looked. But then Geoffrey wrote the truth."

"You knew Geoffrey would meet you and not Mr. C.?"

"Yes. His letters told the truth right away."

"Why didn't you tell me?"

"I was afraid you would tell Uncle Harv and you both would forbid me to come." She paused. "I let Geoffrey know I was an orphan but had an older sister. I told him I was not a rich American, but was poor and worked part-time at the San Francisco immigration office."

Her quick glance at Mary Ellen seemed to mean she had not told him about the inheritance she would have.

"That was wise of you."

"Ahh!" Breanna smiled as if that were quite an accomplishment, being wise.

"I wanted her to get to know me," Geoffrey said. "I've been afraid that when she saw ol' Clay here, she'd dump me. He does favor blonds."

"Oh, Geoffrey. I'm not so shallow." Breanna looked pained. "Besides. I think Mr. C. is too old for me. If he had met me at the dock, I would have told him he was more suited for my sister."

Mary Ellen choked on her tea, reminding her of how she'd choked on her saliva after dreaming of Mr. C. She emitted embarrassing croaking noises, fanned her hot face, and waved away Breanna, who kept asking, "Are you all right?" Mary Ellen finally was able to only repeatedly clear her throat.

While six sets of eyes stared at her, Mr. C. spoke. "I believe Miss Mary Ellen Colson just expressed her opinion of me."

eleven

Clay had never felt so divided. After his parents had died and he'd taken over the main island business, he'd known what to do. His dad had trained him and given him responsibilities, but he'd never had to make any final decisions. So he'd called together the board members, those who knew how his dad thought and acted, and told them he depended on them.

They understood that. The business and their own well-being depended upon the business continuing to run smoothly. With the help of his dad's business associates, the business had prospered.

At stake now was his personal reputation. Seeing Jacob taking responsibility for Geoffrey, Clay wondered what his own dad would have done at a time like this. What would Mak say and do?

Mak was a great one for emphasizing morality based on the teachings of Jesus. Clay had reinforced those principles with Geoffrey. He'd told him they could play the game. As single, fun-loving young men there was nothing wrong with meeting and escorting beautiful young Western women. But he'd stressed it was never about conquest. They had a moral responsibility to treat women with respect.

But the way Geoffrey's thoughtless actions had caused Miss Colson weeks of fear for the safety of her sister raised both moral and legal questions.

"Geoffrey," Jacob said, nodding toward Mary Ellen. "Do you realize that all Miss Colson here has to do is contact the authorities about your tampering with the mail and you can be imprisoned?"

"She wouldn't do that," Breanna said just as Geoffrey scoffed and said, "I did nothing malicious. It was impulsive.

But I wasn't thinking of doing anything illegal. It was a fun thing, like a—" He paused and, after a quick glance at Clay, added, "A harmless game, in a sense."

Clay tried not to show any emotion. Was this the time to admit he was part of that game?

But the current discussion was not about meeting single Western women. That in itself was not illegal or harmful or even underhanded. The women he and Geoffrey had met had been delighted to spend time with them. The fact was, Geoffrey had tampered with the U.S. mail. He had lured a woman to the island under false pretenses, at least initially, and whisked her off to another island.

When and how much is a person supposed to admit?

Mary Ellen Colson already didn't like or trust him. Should he speak up and destroy any possibility of that ever happening? He had a feeling if she knew he was involved, however indirectly, she would, without hesitation, take this to the authorities.

That was different, too. He'd never known a woman—of any age—not to like him as a friend, as a substitute son, or as someone special to her. Never! And a woman had never had the upper hand with him.

Jacob point-blank asked Mary Ellen what she intended to do. Clay wasn't about to look into her eyes. He had the feeling she'd recognize him as less than what he should be. She would see the snowball rolling down the mountainside. Perhaps already in a lump at the bottom.

Glancing at her, he saw that she focused on the table, thoughtful. Finally, she spoke. "I think Geoffrey deserves the chance to prove himself responsible. And Breanna, too. They need to get to know each other better before they jump into... anything more serious."

Jacob and Mary Ellen began to discuss Breanna and Geoffrey as if only the two of them were there. Clay sat back as if he were not involved. Yet Jacob knew he was. Geoffrey knew he was. Matilda and Rose knew he and Geoffrey made a practice of meeting the ships and escorting women. That hadn't been wrong. But now he and Geoffrey had cold ice on their fingers.

"We want to get married," Geoffrey said. "We're of age."

Jacob gave him a cool look. "Legally, yes. But what about maturity? Thinking with a level head? You need to think about this and the possibility of going to jail. To see the error of your ways."

"I can't see that it's an error," Geoffrey said, "except using Clay's photo instead of mine and sneaking the picture in official mail."

"Those were immoral and illegal actions," Jacob said staunchly.

"But it worked out so perfectly. I love Breanna. I don't ever want to look at another woman."

"Do you know what the Bible says about love?"

Geoffrey sighed heavily. "I was raised like you, Jacob. The same parents. In the church. In the mission school. Love is patient. Love is kind. Love is not puffed up."

"Love is action," Jacob added, and Geoffrey acknowledged his words with a nod and a lowering of his gaze.

"Breanna," Mary Ellen said to her downcast sister, "don't you want to plan a wedding instead of jumping into it?"

Clay couldn't help interjecting, "I've seen the wedding dress she's making for you. I can't imagine you'd want to pass that up."

Breanna relented. "You've always been so good to me, Mary Ellen."

Matilda gently rubbed the back of Breanna's hand, soothing her. "It doesn't mean you have to give Geoffrey up. Just get to know him. And get to know Hawaii. This should be the most romantic time of your life. Without your having to cook and clean and shop for a man."

"I wouldn't mind."

"And I'd work my fingers to the bone for her," Geoffrey said.

"I know," Matilda said. "But after a few days of that, all

you'd have is bony fingers."

The two young people glanced at each other and away, as if daunted already.

Matilda brightened. "Take time to enjoy and feel the love so that it grows and can never fade, just like our beautiful flowers on this island. Breanna, be like a lovely flower. And Geoffrey, be the one who tells her about these flowers."

Breanna sighed. "Mary Ellen, I can't believe you would even consider sending my Geoffrey to jail."

Clay saw the sudden moisture that filled Mary Ellen's eyes, heard the way her breath caught before she spoke, as if it hurt to say the words: "Believe it." She rose from her chair, took her cup to the countertop, and stood for a moment. He saw the way her shoulders lifted, the way she squeezed her eyes shut for a moment and took a few breaths before pouring her tea and returning to the table as if she had not just uttered what were probably the most difficult words she'd ever spoken to her sister.

"I think it's settled then," Jacob said. "The conditions of not going to the authorities is that you two get to know each other. Mary Ellen will be the guardian of Breanna. And Clay, if you will, see that Geoffrey holds to his end of the bargain. He works for you most of the time. Would you do that?"

Clay knew what that meant. Although Geoffrey was responsible for his own choices, he and Geoffrey had both played this game with blond Western women. This was Jacob's way of saying it was time for Clay to show his own sense of responsibility. At the same time, Jacob was throwing him right in with this lovely blond Western woman—a woman who didn't care one whit for him.

Clay glanced at Geoffrey and saw a little gleam appear in the boy's eyes. He was likely thinking that with Clay in charge of him, they'd both have their fun and forget all this talk of responsibility. Clay would be easy on him. Much easier than Jacob.

Had Jacob lost his mind?

One look at Jacob, however, revealed that he knew what he was doing.

Clay pretended chagrin. "What all would this entail, Jacob?"

"That you and Mary Ellen chaperone these impulsive young people in lieu of a court case."

Clay gave Mary Ellen Colson his best charming smile and meant for his eyes to express a challenge. "I'm not sure Miss Colson is willing to be escorted around the island by the likes of me."

That was enough to make most women's cheeks color. Many would lower their eyelids and look at him through lowered lashes and say demurely, *Why, Mr. Claybourne Honeycutt, I would be delighted.*

Mary Ellen stared at him for a long moment. He thought her face might have deepened in color but not from pleasure. She turned to Jacob. "If this should be a foursome, could you not be the one to chaperone Geoffrey?"

Jacob shook his head. "I hadn't planned to broach the subject at this time, but I see I must. Before long, I'll be leaving for seminary training on the mainland."

"What?" Geoffrey was surprised.

"We'll talk about it later. Now, we need to get this settled." Jacob turned to Clay. "Will you do this for me, Clay?"

"You know I can't force Geoffrey."

"But you can influence him."

Right. That's what this was all about. Clay's bad influence that had gone too far.

"I will take responsibility for my sister."

Breanna returned her smile. "We could have fun, Mary Ellen. You've never had any always looking after me."

Mary Ellen reached over for her sister's hand that met her halfway across the table. The two had moist eyes.

Geoffrey met Clay's gaze and nodded. Seriously.

Clay looked at Jacob and around at the other women. He could almost read their minds. Finally, a young woman who seemed to consider Claybourne Honeycutt as some kind of villain instead of sweeter than Hawaii's acres and acres of sugarcane.

❧

Long after the scarlet sun dipped into the ocean and the sky changed to sparkling stars and golden moonlight, Mary Ellen listened to Breanna talk about her exciting adventures with Geoffrey in Oahu.

Neither of them could bear for Breanna to go to her own room. They leaned on pillows against the headboard of Mary Ellen's bed.

Mary Ellen loved the closeness of hearing Breanna confide her personal feelings for Geoffrey. Her prayers for Breanna's happiness had been answered. Her sister had someone who adored her and had respected her enough to take her to his parents' home.

"They didn't mind that Geoffrey and I had just met. They understood love at first sight. Oh, Mary Ellen, I don't know if you believe in that."

"I'm beginning to." She didn't add that she also believed in many degrees and kinds of love. She'd had feelings for William but, in retrospect, thought that had simply been the natural process of growing up.

"Geoffrey and I talked about our future. He wants to buy some of the Honeycutt land and run his own sugar business." She sat straighter and faced Mary Ellen. "You'll never guess what I want to do."

"You want to be the world's greatest female surfboarder."

Breanna grabbed her pillow and threw it. Mary Ellen shielded her face with her hands. Laughing with Breanna felt good.

"No, silly. Mrs. Grant took me to the hospital and the orphanage where she volunteers. Now guess."

"You either want to be sick or an orphan."

"Grrr." Breanna rolled her eyes, then became quite serious. "I want to work with orphans. I'll go to college like you said I should. Then, depending on Geoffrey's plans, I will run an orphanage, work in one, or volunteer like Mrs. Grant does. Oh, Mary Ellen, Geoffrey's parents don't have any girls. They would like me as a daughter."

Tears sprung to Mary Ellen's eyes. "I am glad for you. And I do want you to be happy."

Breanna leaned back. "I haven't been this happy since I was little and we had Christmas with Mama and Daddy."

Mary Ellen understood. "Now, tell me all about Oahu."

They settled back on the pillows. Mary Ellen closed her eyes while her sister droned on and on about her exciting life.

She awakened to the flutter of curtains moved by the soft breeze filled with the aroma of exotic flowers. Breanna looked so youthful. Her lips were parted with soft breathing, and her hands were folded on top of the coverlet.

But last night, she'd talked of love and life and goals in a mature way. As proof of her maturity, a short while after awakening, Breanna said, "I want to apologize to the immigration office official."

❧

"I am sorry, and I will volunteer to work for you without pay," Breanna said later that morning. "As I have time."

Mr. Hammeur was quite taken with her and forgave her. "Akemi could use some help with the abundance of picture-bride information that arrived this morning. But I, too, need to apologize."

That surprised Mary Ellen. He had seemed so staid before.

"I should have met you on the dock upon your arrival instead of waiting in my office." He smiled. "To show my good will, Akemi can take two hours for lunch, and she can explain how you might help her."

Mary Ellen realized he did feel guilty about not meeting Breanna and surmised that might explain why he had seemed defensive when she first inquired about her sister.

As they walked down the sidewalk, Mary Ellen looked forward to when she would visit all the shops they passed. Akemi led them into a Japanese restaurant.

In a break in Breanna's conversation while they ate, Mary Ellen asked, "What was your childhood like in Japan, Akemi?"

"My parents were schoolteachers. I was learning some English, too. They talked of the paradise that Japanese men wrote about. In the letters, the men would say, 'Lucky come Hawaii.'"

She smiled at that, but it soon faded. "My parents said we would visit Hawaii someday. I was twelve when they were killed in a village riot. I was in another village with my grandmother. She died when I was fifteen."

Mary Ellen and Breanna said, "I'm so sorry."

"I okay now. I stayed with a family as housekeeper. I learned to cook and clean and sew better. Then a matchmaker made plans for me to come to the beautiful land my parents wanted to visit."

Akemi told Breanna about the man who had sent for her.

"I'm sorry you didn't find love with him," Breanna said.

Akemi shook her head. "I find love. But not with Japanese man."

Mary Ellen and Breanna shared a glance. Akemi didn't elaborate but continued eating.

Mary Ellen ate, too, and watched the two young women becoming fast friends. She felt sure Breanna would soon be told about Akemi's secret love.

This seemed to be the time for young love. . .but not for older sisters to find love.

twelve

In the middle of the week, when he could get away, Clay stopped by to see Jacob. They walked to the church and sat in a pew.

"Jacob, thanks for the suggestion of me and Geoffrey escorting those Colson sisters around the island." He gave a short laugh. "Mary Ellen is something of a challenge."

"Pretty, too."

"She didn't seem to believe that when I mentioned it."

His friend teased, "Maybe she has discernment."

But Clay agreed. "She looks beyond the surface. But I came to talk about Geoffrey."

Jacob's head turned. "What's he doing?"

"Everything he's supposed to. He's always been a good worker for me and Thomas and Mak. He has a carefree spirit. But he is responsible. And. . ." He wanted to be honest. "I think he's really in love with that girl."

"After seeing them together, I can believe that. But it's the illegal thing he did. He took things too far."

"He knows that now."

Jacob nodded. "Maybe I carried this too far, trying to make Geoffrey prove he's responsible. When I lectured him about responsibility, perhaps I was talking to myself."

"Yourself?"

When Jacob hesitated, Clay said, "Hey. There was a time when we could tell each other anything. Everything."

Clay followed Jacob's gaze to the front of the church and the cross on the distant wall. He spoke as if to someone other than Clay. "I've fallen in love with a Japanese girl. How can I have an effective ministry if I even think of pursuing a relationship with her? Or making her an outcast to her own race?"

112

Several things fell into place. Jacob's strange behavior had been motivated by his trying to avoid Akemi. "Is God telling you not to pursue her? Or are you concerned about prejudiced people?"

"It would harm the ministry. It would change our culture."

"Akemi is different."

"Yes. But she is Japanese. Only a few break out of the work force. You know that."

Clay gave an ironic laugh. "But she has. Everyone loves her."

"Yes. But she would be scorned by her people and by many Caucasians if we marry. How could I do such a thing to her?" He scoffed. "She is nineteen. I am twenty-nine. She respects me. How can I think she would consider me? She did not accept the man who paid her passage from Japan. She turned down the son of the Japanese restaurant owners. How can I think—"

"Why did she turn them down?"

"She said she does not love them. That she does not think like a picture bride. But I have been her schoolteacher. Her Bible teacher."

"Jacob, you'll drive yourself loco trying to figure this out. Tell God the desires of your heart and let Him handle it. I've seen how she looks at you. She has feelings for you."

"She has feelings for everybody, Clay. Since she's asked Jesus into her heart, she shines. She can't get enough of life and faith. She wants to share that with her Japanese brothers and sisters."

"And what kind of woman would God want you to have as a minister's wife?"

Jacob didn't answer. He didn't need to. God would want a woman devoted to Him. A woman of faith excited about her Christian life and eager to share it.

Strange, how he could give advice to Jacob about life and love and God. Clay had never seriously considered a wife. But if he did, he'd want one like he'd just described.

But would that kind of woman want him?

He laid his hand on Jacob's shoulder. "I know how you fee The thought of love can knock a person senseless, like bein pushed under by a wave, getting caught in the undertov coming up to take a breath, and getting slammed in the hea by the surfboard."

Jacob drew back. "That bad, huh?"

Clay shrugged. "So I've heard."

It was good to have a laugh with Jacob. "I want to ask yo something. Why is the church steeple one hundred feet high?

"Take a brochure that's in the foyer. Figure it out."

Jacob didn't make things easy.

"And do what you want with Geoffrey," he said. "You wi anyway."

Clay grinned and said aloha to his friend. Outside, h looked up at the steeple, then stuck the folded brochure int his pocket.

Riding along the streets of Hilo, lifting his hand to thos walking and on horseback, he thought about Geoffrey. Th decision of what to do about him wasn't really his, but Mar Ellen Colson's. She was the one who could bring charge against Geoffrey. He should talk with her.

He parked a couple of shops away from the dress shop an walked down the street. Standing at the side of the displa window, he looked inside.

This wasn't the first time he'd done that. His first glimps had been when he wondered what kind of trick that woma was playing on him. He'd watched her sewing little pearls o a wedding dress. Then he'd confronted her, and she'd stoo up to him, suspicious and accusatory and without a smile.

He smiled, seeing her now. That's how she should b instead of worrying about a sister old enough to make he own decisions. She was wearing a *holoku*. She was laughin and her eyes seemed filled with joy. Perhaps she had begun get into the Hawaiian relaxed, carefree lifestyle.

But she hadn't yet let her hair down.

During much of the morning, Mary Ellen sewed seed pearls onto the wedding dress and listened to how Pilar talked about the clothing and related to customers. When they were alone, Pilar talked about her life in Texas, contrasting it to a new beginning in Hawaii.

"What was your life like in San Francisco?" she asked.

Talking about the shock of her parent's sudden death and the devastation to San Francisco seemed to release a burden in Mary Ellen that she hadn't known she carried.

Then Pilar confided about her own life. She had lived in Oahu. "Clay's sister and I are best friends. We went to nursing school together. Susanne became a pediatrician, married a doctor, and has a family. I married a doctor, too, but. . ." She paused. "After he died of tuberculosis—"

"Oh, I'm sorry."

Pilar smiled sadly. "I was blessed to have a good life with him. I try to focus on the good. After he died, I moved back here to be with Matilda and her niece, Jane, who are like family."

Mary Ellen felt warmth in her heart, thinking of Matilda and Rose, who were in back, unpacking a recent shipment. "They treat me and Breanna like we're their own."

Pilar nodded. "They're like that."

The bell tinkled, and while Pilar helped the woman who entered the shop, Mary Ellen thought about family. Although Breanna talked about missing Geoffrey terribly, Mary Ellen loved every moment of her time with her sister. She liked seeing her and Akemi walking up the sidewalk, talking and laughing. They would knock on the dress shop window and wave at her. Sometimes, Mary Ellen went to lunch with them.

As if her thinking made them materialize, the two girls came back from lunch and into the shop just as Matilda came out from the back with a couple of dresses and laid them on the countertop. Rose pushed in a mannequin on wheels.

Matilda held out a dress. "Try this on, Mary Ellen. Let's see how it looks."

In the dressing room, she felt like a different person wearing something brighter than the bland colors she'd worn at work. The dress fell loosely from the bodice. Cream-colored eyelet bordered the overlay falling a few inches from the shoulders and down from the scooped neckline. The overlay rounded halfway down the back, resembling a shawl.

She joined the others. "I love it. This color reminds me of last night's sunset when the sky was pinkish-orange."

"It's coral." Matilda touched the trim. "This eyelet sets it off perfectly. Now, how does it feel?"

"Light. Airy. Comfortable."

"That's the point," Matilda said. "This is Hawaii's version of the European tea gown."

"The first one, similar to this, came about at the request of Queen Kalakua," Rose said. "She loved the missionary women's clothing when they came here in 1820 and asked, or demanded, the wives make her a dress like theirs out of white cambric."

"This one is more formal." Pilar held up the white one. "It's fine white cotton."

Matilda touched it. "Our queens and princesses wore these for informal occasions. For formal occasions, they wore the latest European fashions."

Rose said she was going to put the cotton dress on the mannequin for the display window.

"The Hawaiian people wanted a Western look with the loose, comfortable feel," Matilda said. "That's why this style is called holoku."

"Holoku," Mary Ellen said. "I'll need to remember that in case a customer asks."

"Western women like the explanations," Pilar said.

"Will they ask what holoku means?" Mary Ellen asked.

"They will be as interested in that as you just indicated," Matilda said. "There are two versions of the story. One is tha when the native seamstresses sewed their dresses they said *holo* when they turned the wheel to start the sewing machine. They said *ku* when they stopped at the end of a seam. *Holo* means *go* and *ku* means *stop*."

"That's interesting," Mary Ellen said, "I can hardly wait for the next one."

Matilda obliged them. "When the Hawaiian women wore the dresses for the first time, they said 'We can run in it; we can stand.' They were not restricted by tight or binding clothes."

"I understand," Mary Ellen said. "I could float or dance in this." She made a fancy dance step like girls did at the orphanage when having fun. The others clapped rhythmically for her.

Just then, the bell tinkled.

She stopped abruptly.

Mr. C.'s dark eyes looked her over and gave them all a quizzical glance. "If I'd known there was to be a performance, I'd have come sooner."

Realizing she still held the sides of the dress, Mary Ellen let go and smoothed it.

"The new shipment of holokus," Matilda said. "What do you think?"

His glance slid to Mary Ellen again. "Quite attractive." He walked to the wedding dress. "But this is my idea of an eye-catching dress." He reached out.

"No," Mary Ellen said, louder than she meant. "I'm sorry. But the oil from hands will cause the seed pearls to change from their natural color."

"What a pity," he mused. "Such a beautiful creation. . . untouchable."

thirteen

The outing Mr. C. had suggested of seeing the plantation
and sights of Hawaii with Breanna and Geoffrey had to be
postponed.

On Monday morning, he stopped in to say a wire had been
received that picture brides would arrive by the end of the
week.

Mary Ellen was excited about that and began asking
questions.

"A lot goes into this over a long period of time. We can talk
about it if you'd like to help me at the immigration office."

"What about Akemi and Breanna?"

"They had the option of buying personal items for the
brides or helping with files."

"I can guess their choice."

His smile was wide, and he nodded.

"I am interested in the picture brides, particularly after
meeting Akemi, but. . ." She glanced at Pilar.

"Go on," Pilar said. "Your volunteer status here means you
come and go as you please."

"It's payment enough to learn about fashion and to meet
the customers." Mary Ellen's Hawaiian experience had not
extended beyond working at the shop, exploring the town of
Hilo, and taking walks on the beach. But those activities alone
were like a fragrant breath of fresh air after having spent so
many years in an orphanage, a boardinghouse, and an office.

Just walking from the dress shop to the immigration office
with a man was more exciting than riding a cable car in San
Francisco. "What happened to the Japanese man who deceived
Akemi?"

"I told him he'd be deported on the next ship to Japan.

But first, I took him to Akemi to apologize. She mentioned a widowed aunt who would like a man like Ke. Hoping that would ease Akemi's distress, I went along with it."

The conversation halted when a horse and carriage came alongside them and slowed as the driver greeted them. Mary Ellen had not met one unfriendly person in Hawaii. Aloha was beginning to come natural to her.

"And what happened?"

He shrugged. "Nothing unusual. He just spoke."

She gave him her best exasperated look. "With Akemi's aunt and Ke?"

He grinned down at her, and she knew he had teased her.

"Ke went through the proper procedure, and the widow arrived. They're married, and are among my best workers, along with being leaders in the village. That can happen when you give someone a second chance."

She glanced up quickly, but he seemed focused on the ocean ahead of them. Was he trying to tell her she should give Geoffrey a second chance?

Mr. Hammeur already had the records in a room where Mr. C. could review them.

"What I do," Clay explained after they went behind the desk on which folders were stacked, "is put each worker's and bride's forms together, along with their photos. Check for complete and correct information. After the brides arrive, if we find any discrepancy—as in the case of Ke—the bride should be returned to the ship and my worker deported."

Mary Ellen nodded. She'd worked with similar procedures in San Francisco.

"Also look for full payments. In the past when workers were on a payment plan, many stopped making payments after the marriage. That led to more stress and less work getting done."

The work wasn't complicated; it simply required meticulous checking of many items. Mary Ellen checked the brides' forms while Mr. C. checked his workers, and then they combined them.

"You know what you're doing," Mr. C. complimented.

She glanced at him. "It's not exactly deep-sea fishing."

He conceded that with a nod. "Mr. Hammeur will be grateful that you, instead of he, reviewed the forms. So much so that if you decide to file charges against Geoffrey, Mr. Hammeur will favor you and testify against your sister's beau."

"Then Geoffrey should be doing this to get into the good graces of Mr. Hammeur."

"I thought of that. But then I said to myself, 'Self, which do you want more—Geoffrey in the good graces of Mr. Hammeur, or yourself in the good graces of Miss Colson?'"

"This," she mocked playfully, "is supposed to put you in my good graces?"

"Whoa." He grimaced. "Guess I got that one wrong. I'll try and come up with something else. You're mighty hard to please."

Mary Ellen reached for another form and photo. No, she really wasn't. Working in the Hawaii immigration office beside Mr. C. was a sight more appealing than the lonely office in San Francisco. Strange, how a man's presence could make a menial chore seem like the most important thing at the moment.

But then, wasn't that a trademark of Mr. Claybourne Honeycutt? Making women feel that being near him was all any woman could dream of? She preferred not to dwell on such a thought.

She remembered when Breanna had laid her picture beside Mr. C.'s and Mary Ellen had thought them to be a most attractive couple who could belong to each other. Now, looking at the pictures of men and women, she could visualize them together, too.

"Something wrong?"

She realized she'd stared long at a picture. "Sorry. No, my mind wandered. I was thinking that if I didn't know better, I'd believe these couples already belonged together. But I do notice something."

"What's that?"

"The eyes. Almost all the men seem to have an uncertain look. The brides have a hopeful and excited expression in their eyes."

"The French have a saying: *Les yeux sont le miroir de l'âme.*"

Ah, classroom French. "The eyes are the mirror of the soul."

He turned to her. "I wonder, if I looked into your eyes right now, what would I learn about your soul?"

She focused on the papers, determined not to indicate she found him the slightest bit appealing. To become like a silly infatuated schoolgirl would be humiliating.

Of course, she wasn't infatuated.

What could she say about her eyes? Let him look into them? What would she see in his? She had already seen the daring, the challenge as if to ask if any woman could resist him.

Pray. *Lord, help me.* As if in answer, she thought of something. "I remember a Bible verse saying that the light of the body is in the eye."

"What does that mean?"

"Um," she hedged. "I think it means you can sometimes tell if a person has light or darkness in them."

"Hmmm. Do you suppose some of your light might seep into the darkness of my soul, Miss Colson, if you were to look deep into my eyes?"

She didn't know if he taunted or jested. But she was not about to look into his eyes or allow him to look into hers. Her soul, her heart, her mind, her good sense seemed in turmoil so much of the time. Perhaps it was due to the voyage over a churning ocean, or the swaying of palms, or the constant trade winds. In San Francisco, her life had seemed so static, so controlled. Here, it felt like sifting sand. She wasn't sure of her footing.

No, she couldn't let him see her uncertainty. "Let's finish this," she said. "I'd like to get back to the shop."

She worked with the files representing people committing

to spend the rest of their lives together. The men worked so hard. The women traveled so far, in the hope of finding love.

And with few exceptions, they found it through the most unlikely of things: a photo.

❧

"Today, you get to see the picture brides," Matilda said, while she, Rose, Breanna, and Akemi put the baskets of personal items in the wagon.

Mary Ellen felt the excitement of seeing how the couples would react when they first met. Would they be mistaken about their true love like Breanna had been about Mr. C.? Would they feel like Breanna did about Geoffrey? Would they be special to each other?

Soon, they stood on the sandy dock, their heads turning at the sound of the train coming down the rails.

Mr. C. exited, followed by Japanese men in dark suits and white shirts, wearing their hair slicked back. They looked much like they had in the photos, except one. "Why is that one wearing a hat?"

Matilda shrugged. "He may be the only one who could afford a hat."

Twenty men shifted uncomfortably on the sand until Clay had them line up. They then stood like statues with gazes fixed on the ocean.

Mary Ellen guessed the anxiety they must be feeling, remembering her anxiety about meeting Mr. C. even after she thought Breanna would be his bride. These men were committed to a lifetime with a woman they'd never met in person.

Geoffrey was last to exit the train, along with a couple of men who gave each worker the photo of his bride.

"Rose and I will take their leis," Matilda said. They struck off with the baskets of colorful, flowered necklaces.

Akemi said, "When I arrived as a bride, the men had leis but the brides did not get baskets. We had only what we could bring. Matilda and Rose started the practice of helping picture brides feel welcome. Maybe because I felt so lost and sad. See, God makes good comes from the worst things."

Mary Ellen smiled at Akemi, impressed with the young girl's positive attitude.

Clay and Geoffrey walked up with Matilda and Rose.

"The men dress nicely," Mary Ellen said.

"They want to look their best," Matilda said. "But they have only one suit. Sometimes a suit is borrowed or rented. It's worn when they have their pictures taken so that the matchmaker in Japan can see they look nice. The same suit is worn for weddings and funerals."

Geoffrey laughed. "Clay and I used to say why not? They're one and the same." He looked at Breanna. "That's before I met the most wonderful girl in the world."

"For your information, Miss Colson," Clay said, "this is a small part of the work Geoffrey does. Most of the work is in the fields."

Geoffrey added, "I plan to start saving. Clay says I could buy one of his small fields if I show enough responsibility to manage one. I can do that."

"I know you can do anything you set your mind to, Geoffrey," Breanna said.

"For you, I can."

Mary Ellen watched them stare into each other's eyes. She glanced at Mr. C. He shook his head and looked out to sea. That seemed to confirm his opinion of love.

"The Japanese men look scared to death," Mary Ellen said.

Clay laughed. "Those men have worked for years to buy a wife. They've saved, had their photos taken, bought or rented their suits, paid the passage for the bride. Now they must be wondering what kind of woman they're going to live with for the rest of their lives and if it is all worth it."

"It's not only the men who are scared," Akemi said. "I know. I traveled across the ocean with hopes of a wonderful life with a man I would learn to love. But none of us expected to be like Breanna and Geoffrey. Our homeland is very poor.

Our young men went away to make their fortunes in this place they had heard was paradise."

Mary Ellen was curious. "How did you know who to be matched with?"

"The men's photos came to the matchmaker's office or the immigration office. On the request form, the man tells his age, what part of Japan he came from, which island he is working on in Hawaii. He tells if he is very religious, how much education, and any special gifts. The matchmaker knows the bride's information. But mostly we only have the photos to go by. The matchmaker tries to see what is in the face and eyes of the man in the photo."

"Photos can be deceiving, can they not, Miss Colson?" Clay asked.

What did he expect her to say about his photo? "Apparently, Mr. C., Akemi was deceived by a man twenty years older than his photo. The one sent to the office in San Francisco was even more deceptive. It was the wrong man and sent in an illegal way."

Akemi spoke up. "Oh, but like I say, God makes good come from everything. I did not think so when I saw the man who was to be my husband. But God allowed that bad thing so good could come." She smiled at Mr. C. "And Clay has changed so many things for his workers and their brides. God has used him in such good ways."

"I don't know how good that is, Akemi." Clay's voice sounded abrupt. "They're not brought here for a romantic adventure. They're here to work and help the men be more content with their work and lives. They're brides, yes, but they're also my employees."

"They know that, Mr. Clay," she said. "But it's good to give them one good day of romance."

It sounded as if he mumbled, "Women," then gestured toward the docking area.

Mary Ellen saw Billy nod and come toward them with a rolling cart.

"Oh, we'd better get a move on," Matilda said. "The ship is docking."

❧

After boarding the ship, Mary Ellen stood outside the door where the baskets were placed. Chatter inside the room where the picture brides were ceased when Clay walked into the room. He welcomed the women as brides for his workers and as his employees who had come to work in the sugarcane.

"That's the *luna*," Akemi said of the woman translating his words. "She make many trips with brides."

He came out and nodded at Matilda. Looking as serious as his tone of voice had sounded, he left the ship. Mary Ellen could understand that the brief encounter would cause the women to think about life after a wedding. She hoped the message got through to Breanna, too.

A hush again fell over the cabin when Mary Ellen and the others entered. The middle-aged luna bowed and spoke in broken English.

One of the picture brides looked to be in her late twenties and two others in their early twenties, but the rest appeared to be no more than fifteen or sixteen years old.

"They look scared," Mary Ellen whispered to Matilda.

"They are. Without money, they can't return to Japan. The men pay their passage."

Akemi walked to the middle of the floor. "Do any speak English?"

"I Shizue," said a heavy-set girl, quite different from the thin, short ones. "I speak little. I get point across." Most of the girls giggled.

The oldest one rose from the corner, tall and serious. Her hair hung over one shoulder. She bowed. "I am Kohana. I speak Japanese, Chinese, and little English."

Shizue nodded. "She teach us on the voyage."

Several began saying words they thought were English. "Aloha, thank you, good meet you, yes, no."

Akemi asked questions in Japanese and received answers. Then she turned to Mary Ellen and the other women. "The girls have already washed and dressed in their finest, other than their wedding dresses." Akemi had them sit on the wooden storage benches around the wall.

Matilda said, "She will tell her story in English and in Japanese."

Akemi related her experience of disappointment, but also the wonder of learning about Christianity and having Jesus in her heart.

Most of the girls looked at their hands folded on their kimonos. "You will not be forced to be Christian," Akemi said. "But you will hear it."

She told them that she knew the luna had warned that they now belonged to the man who paid their passage. She told them that had changed and they could report any mistreatment. "Your boss, Mr. Honeycutt, is good and kind."

Matilda returned Mary Ellen's glance and smiled.

Now Akemi was telling the brides that with few exceptions there were no jobs for Japanese women. But Matilda and Rose had made it their project to help any who had misgivings about the man they were contracted to marry.

"What if he not look good, like his picture?" asked Shizue.

The women began to talk at once.

The luna held up her hands for silence. "Everything will be explained." She nodded to Matilda who said, "We can give the baskets now."

Mary Ellen felt their joy as they smiled and laughed. In the baskets were all sorts of items any girl would want, including lotions, soaps, hairbrushes, decorative combs, a little mirror, and other personal items.

Kohana stepped to a mirror on the wall. She made an elaborate hair arrangement on the top of her head, using decorative combs from the basket.

Shizue paced. "I will not marry a man if he no suit me."

Akemi began telling how lucky they were that things had

changed. "Marriages used to be performed at the immigration office the day picture brides arrived. Miss Matilda and Miss Rose now have you meet the men. You will stay at the inn. Then you will see where the men work and meet the people in the village. After that, you will prepare for your wedding day."

They seemed fearful, and eager, to walk down the gangplank to the beach. The captain checked the names and papers of each girl as she left the ship. Each carried her basket and photo of her contracted husband.

"We will stay near them," Matilda said. "They need to know we're supportive because the luna will return to Japan after the wedding."

The men had separated into three groups. Geoffrey and the other Caucasian men stood behind the grooms. Farther down, dockworkers looked on, and Mary Ellen recognized the uniform of immigration officers.

Clay walked up. "Now," he said, "we get to observe what happens when arranged love meets reality."

Akemi said, "The day I refused the older man, he dropped the lei on the sand and bent head. He walk to train with shoulders slumped. These men look okay young."

"The one on the end could be in his thirties."

"That one for Kohana."

Mary Ellen remembered putting their files together.

The brides and workers were studying their photos, making sure who belonged to whom.

The thirty-year-old man seemed so serious. Perhaps he expected to be rejected. "This must be embarrassing," Mary Ellen said.

Akemi expressed surprise. "No. It is honor. They offer hearts and lives to each other. It is good."

All the Japanese men were thin except the one wearing a hat. He was short and had an abundant abdomen.

Shizue walked up to him. The top of his hat reached almost to the top of her head. She frowned, her head bobbing as she looked from the photo to him several times. "Fumio?"

Off came his hat as he bowed deeply, revealing a bald spot on top of his head.

Shizue began to laugh and pointed at him. "Okay, Fumio. You have hat, but you not richer than others. You balder."

"So much brains push out hair."

"Careful." She touched her hair, and he grimaced. "You don't look like much, but. . ." She looked at the form in her hand. "You better sing."

He bellowed out a song in Japanese, making others laugh. Shizue put her hands on her hips. "Fumio, my name means quiet inlet. You better know I'm more like a—"

"Tsunami?"

"Exactly."

"Yippee. Just the kind of woman I want." Before she could lean forward for it, he had the lei over her head and hanging from her neck. He plopped the hat on his head and wore a big smile.

Shizue reached into her basket and brought out a long thread and a folded fan.

Akemi explained. "The linen thread means gray hair of old age. The fan can spread out to show future wealth and many children. Now they are engaged."

The others were becoming engaged in the same way.

Others were exchanging names and bowing. Some smiled boldly, some timidly, but each seemed to accept the other. Except the tall ones on the end, who were talking.

"I have a goal, Kohana," the man said in English. "I save. I will someday have my own land."

"I, too, have a goal, Miyamoto," Kohana said with equal pride. "On that land I will plant a garden and write a book about Japanese gardening."

"I have many books." He lifted the lei.

Kohana bent her head for the lei. She gave him the thread and fan. He stepped back, with his hands folded in front of him. Kohana stepped back and looked off down the beach as if studying the place that was now her new home.

"The women will go to the inn now," Matilda said. "We have a big room on the second floor and cots so they can stay together to prepare for their wedding. Most bring their wedding dresses with them. Some could not afford them."

She nodded toward Clay. "Just as Clay makes sure the men all have suits, Rose and I make sure the brides have wedding dresses."

"But you need to know," Clay said, "these are laborers from another country. They're not accepted into the general population. They're not U.S. citizens. They are under contract for work."

"He's right," Matilda said. "He's gone out of his way to accommodate them. But they're here to work, and he's not even under any obligation to allow the workers to have brides."

"Then why do you?" Mary Ellen looked up at him.

"The men are better workers when married and with children, instead of being bunked with hundreds of other men."

"They all seem pleased," Rose said. Mary Ellen followed her gaze to where the luna was grouping the brides together. Geoffrey had gathered their contracts.

"The men can refuse the women, too," Matilda said, "but I don't know of that having happened, do you, Clay?"

"No," he said. "None of my men have refused the match made for them that started with nothing more than a photo. Women are harder to please, I guess."

"Or just more discerning," Mary Ellen said and regretted her words immediately. She'd never known anyone to bring out the worst in her like Mr. C. managed to.

"That's how someone described you." He grinned at Mary Ellen and walked toward the men being led to the train.

fourteen

Chairs had been set along one wall of the spacious dining
hall in the Japanese village at the sugarcane plantation. Clay
sat in the center with Matilda and Mary Ellen on each side
of him.

"The wedding ceremony will take place along the wall
opposite us," Matilda explained.

"Let's move our chairs in front of them," Breanna said to
Akemi, "so we don't have to lean in to hear what they're saying."
They did.

"I don't often come to these ceremonies," Clay said. "For
the past two years, Matilda, Rose, and Akemi have. Wives
of my foremen help. The owners of two Japanese restaurants
bring their cooks and prepare the food."

Mary Ellen looked at the adjacent wall where Rose and
two other white women and several Japanese women in
colorful kimonos worked at long tables with white cloths,
flowers, and dishes.

"Do the other workers come to the wedding?"

"No. If that were allowed, they'd be attending weddings all
the time instead of working. But they have their good times
with their own religious traditions, music, dancing, and games."
He said what Akemi had earlier. "We can't force them to be
Christian. We can only influence them by showing Christian
love."

"Is that why you let them have this ceremony?"

"No. My brother doesn't do it this way. His workers and
their brides are married soon after they dock in Oahu. I let this
happen because Matilda and Rose talked me into it. It's their
project, and they pay the Japanese restaurant owners in town
to provide the wedding feast."

"That's good of you to allow this special day."

"I don't know," he said. "They seem to appreciate it. I try to respect their culture. You see, the early missionaries didn't respect the culture of the Hawaiians. They saw them as heathen because they wore little or no clothing. And they considered Hawaiians sinful to move their bodies in a hula dance. Much of their culture was lost."

Matilda added to that. "The businesses and politics here are run by descendants of those missionaries. They became wealthy while the native Hawaiians became poorer. Why, not too many years ago I was partying with the king. Now, Hawaii is annexed to the U.S., and royalty has been replaced by Westernized politicians."

"But we are beginning to see the value of the Hawaiian culture and appreciate their history," Clay said. "When I say *we*, I'm not referring just to me personally. Hawaiians are being appreciated again. And we're beginning to see that Hawaii's uniqueness is in the many nationalities and cultures."

Akemi turned. "Jacob said most of Hawaii is Christian."

Clay agreed. "The missionaries made some mistakes, but two-thirds of Hawaii is now Christian."

Breanna spoke over her shoulder. "Are those two preachers?"

A man in a black suit had entered and stood in the middle of the platform near the front.

"Not preachers," Clay said. "The seated one is a Japanese priest from the temple in Hilo. The one standing is a civil official. This is not a Christian ceremony."

Matilda said, "This is a combination of Japanese, Western, and Hawaiian."

Twenty men entered in their black suits and lined up on in two rows, looking as stiff as they had when awaiting their brides at the dock.

Akemi looked back and spoke softly. "In Japan, if the man could afford it, or borrow it, he would wear a black silk kimono."

"Do they feel badly about not wearing a kimono?"

"No. They know they are in the United States, so this okay. The women know it, too. But wait. You see the women."

"Look," Matilda whispered.

Mary Ellen drew in her breath at the lovely parade of women entering the dining hall from the far end of the room. They wore white silk kimonos. Their faces were painted creamy white, contrasting with their dark eyes and upswept hairstyles fastened with tortoiseshell combs.

The civil official said something to the men. The luna stood aside as if ready to coach if needed. But each groom seemed to know to whom he belonged.

"The white means a beginning and an end," Matilda said.

"Just like aloha means hello and good-bye," Clay added.

Akemi nodded. "The bride wears white because she 'dies as her father's daughter and is reborn into her husband's life."

When the man approached his bride, he bowed. The luna said something, and the woman bent slightly. The man put a white and purple lei over his bride's head.

"Those are white and purple orchids," Akemi said. "In Japan, purple is the color of love. The iris is a favored flower."

"What is our color of love?" Breanna said.

"The red rose is a symbol of love," Matilda said. "Then there's the white dress for a wedding."

Mary Ellen patted Breanna's shoulder. "Like the one I'm making for you."

Breanna touched Mary Ellen's hand, then spoke to Akemi. "Did they practice that ritual?"

Akemi answered. "They do not practice. They be very careful to hear what the official and the luna say."

"With few exceptions," Clay said, "the Japanese are very meticulous in all they do, in work and particularly in personal cleanliness."

"Now," Akemi said. "They will honor the spirits. The priest waves a branch called a *harai-gushi*. That is to bless the couples."

They moved as couples to a table where each groom drank from a small cup, then handed it to the bride. They did that three times.

Mary Ellen touched Akemi's shoulder as a signal she wanted an explanation.

"There are three cups," Akemi said. "Each larger than the other. That is called *san san kudo*. The groom takes three sips from a cup, and then the bride takes three sips. That is nine sips each. Nine is lucky number because it cannot be divided by two. So they are now becoming one."

Next was the rosary. Akemi explained that, too. There were twenty-one beads of two different colors. Eighteen beads represented the couple, two represented each family, and one represented the Buddha. "All of the beads on one string," she said, "means the couple and their families are joined, even though their families are in Japan."

The ceremony ended, and a photographer appeared. Clay explained to Mary Ellen there would be a group picture, and one of the couple pictures would be for the official records. "I think I'll take my leave," he said.

"You know we can join them for the wedding feast," Matilda said.

"I never have," Clay said.

"Why?" Mary Ellen asked.

The first thing that crossed his mind was, "I'm the owner. They're my workers."

"Don't they know that?"

"Sure."

"Then what are you conveying by not eating with them? Is there some significance to that?"

He looked at the ceiling. That word again. She'd used it when asking about the church steeple. Did there have to be significance to everything? Some things just. . .were.

Matilda spoke up. "You've never too old to change."

Tripping over Clay's mind was the question, *Claybourne Honeycutt change?*

What would it hurt to stay for the meal?

The priest stood at the head of the tables. Clay moved to the opposite head. Matilda and Rose moved to his left. "You and Breanna are special guests today," he said, "sit here." Mary Ellen sat next to him on his right, next Breanna, then Akemi.

With amusement, he watched Mary Ellen and Breanna exchange glances over the plates of fish. The head and tail had been formed into a circle. "That is the symbol of eternity," Matilda said. She laughed at their wide eyes indicating they were unsure about the fish.

"And the clams served with two halves is symbolic of the newly married couple," Akemi said.

The brides and grooms came to the table and remained standing. The priest said an invocation and blessed them again. When he finished, all the men turned toward Clay and bowed. Seeing that, the women did, too.

Clay figured Miss Colson would not like that, but his quick glance revealed her looking around at them as if she were pleased about everything.

He gestured for them to sit. "This is your day," he said. "I will give a gift to each of you."

He hadn't thought of that before. But people do change. While his words were being translated, or those who understood were thanking him, he mumbled to Mary Ellen. "What should I give?" He leaned over for her answer.

"You said they love cleanliness. What about soap or candles or something that smells sweet for the woman. Maybe a little money for the men?"

"Excellent," he whispered. Aloud he said. "Your gifts will be delivered to you tomorrow morning." He almost added, "not too early," but realized in time that might not be well-received by Miss Colson and some of the others.

He sat. Mary Ellen looked at him and smiled. For the first time, she smiled at him. Did she, for an instant, like him?

People can change. . . .

While they ate, Mary Ellen and Breanna discussed the beauty of the wedding. He could readily see it didn't hurt a thing to show some special kindness to his workers. Then he wondered if he heard Breanna correctly.

"I've decided I want a different kind of wedding."

Mary Ellen's hand returned the forkful of food to her plate. Breanna continued about the kind of wedding she wanted. "A Hawaiian one. On the beach. In a Hawaiian kind of dress. Like Matilda and Rose said Jane and Mak had."

Breanna didn't know it, but she had just broken her sister's heart. Mary Ellen's stark face reminded him of the white-faced Japanese women. They would wash the white from their faces and tomorrow would wear hats in the fields to keep the sun from turning them brown or red. What could rid Breanna's sister of her disappointment?

He glanced at Matilda, who returned his look with a knowing smile. She knew the love and time Mary Ellen had put into that dress. Now he wondered what she would do after Breanna married Geoffrey. Remain in Hawaii? Could he and she have no differences between them and be. . .friends?

Friends with that beautiful blond Westerner who did not particularly like or trust him?

He thought not.

At least, not friends. . .only.

◆

They were having breakfast when Breanna asked, "Do you mind if I pick another wedding dress?"

Since yesterday, Mary Ellen had known this question was coming. She spoke honestly. "Every bride should have the dress she wants."

"Do you want to m—"

"Why don't you come to the dress shop?" Mary Ellen interrupted. She would not make another wedding dress for Breanna. "Matilda and Rose can help us look in the catalogs and find what you want."

"I didn't want to be at the office anyway without Akemi. Jacob is leaving this morning, and she's seeing him off. Geoffrey will be there, too." She sighed heavily, then smiled. "But I can't see him without you."

Half the morning was taken up with their poring over catalogs. The silk kimonos had influenced Breanna. "I'd like something silk and soft and flowing. Oh, like this."

They all agreed the one she had chosen was lovely. The simple lines were similar to the tea gowns. Sheer, flowing drapes fell gracefully over the shoulder and down into the moderate-length train. Mary Ellen could imagine Breanna slipping her fingers in the small ribbon loops on the drapes and making dainty dance steps while turning in sweeping motions of delight.

The drapes could be removed, revealing the narrow straps of the dress that was lined with China silk.

Breanna moaned. "Look at the price."

"That's all right," Mary Ellen said. "I told you I would provide your wedding dress."

Breanna hugged her. "You're so good to me." She stood back and glanced at the dress on the form. "You really don't mind?"

Mary Ellen tapped the catalog. "This is you."

Akemi stopped in later and asked the two sisters to lunch with her. While eating, Akemi said, "I could not let Jacob leave without saying I love him."

Breanna leaned forward. "What did he say?"

"He say I am young, should find Japanese man and have five children. He say if he had a right, he would ask me to wait, but he had no right." She shook her head. "I told him that while he is gone, I will go to college and be ready to help him when he returns."

"What did he say?" Mary Ellen and Breanna both asked.

"That I should not sacrifice my life for him." Her smile was precious. "But I say, it would be my pleasure. He say he write to me." She paused. "If he marries someone else, I will go to Japan and suffer. I could not be on the same island with him. It would be hard being in the same world with him, without him."

Mary Ellen was speechless for a long moment. Finally she said, "I will pray." Exactly what she would say in her prayer, she didn't know. But she would pray.

After lunch, she stood beside the white wedding gown. She touched the satin and lace, but not the pearls. A dress with thousands of seed pearls, hand sewn, lovingly made.

She felt a tear.

The bell tinkled. She blinked to dry her teary eyes. She turned. Clay stood in the doorway. He walked up to her. "Would you have dinner with me? At a hotel. We should talk about Breanna and Geoffrey. Say, seven o'clock?"

Matilda, who was dressing a mannequin, turned to them. Mary Ellen had no idea why Clay winked at Matilda. She laughed and waved. "Get out of here," she said.

After he left, Matilda said, "Let's find you the perfect outfit to wear."

"I didn't even say I'd go. But no thank you on the outfit. This is about Breanna and Geoffrey, not like we're"—she decided to use Matilda's words—"out on the town or anything."

Matilda scolded. "You're going out with Hawaii's sugar king, our most ineligible bachelor, and I'm sure you've noticed how heads turn just to look at him."

Mary Ellen glanced away.

"Except yours, of course," Matilda added.

She laughed. "I'm not blind."

"Then let's dress you up to match him. That doesn't mean you can't talk about business."

She agreed, not wanting to look frumpy and embarrass him.

Matilda went in back and returned with a box. "Let's go home and get you ready. If we need a tuck or two, we can manage that."

Shortly before seven, Mary Ellen picked up the deep pink dress, still as awed by its beauty as when she'd taken it from the box. It had fit perfectly. Now, Matilda helped her slip into it. The silk floated down her body and fell easily to her feet where the material was fuller for walking freedom.

"Look in the mirror," Matilda said.

Mary Ellen could hardly believe what a dress could do. She'd never worn such a low neckline, but in the V was a lovely lace insert. A wide row of glass beads and sequins adorned the neckline from the shoulders to below the lace. The beads came together in a large cluster. Two-inch delicate strands of glass hung from the cluster.

She touched the ruffle of gathered silk on the sheer sleeve that reached her elbow. The skirt had an overlay of pink net. A row of glass beads traveled down one side of the dress to a third of the way from the bottom. The net was gathered to form a graceful loop over the silk and was adorned with a cluster of beads.

"I've never worn a dress like this. It's so elegant."

Matilda agreed. "It will fit in wherever Clay takes you. It's perfect for evening or very formal."

"Now, my hair."

"Your natural wave is lovely, and long hair suits you." Matilda tapped her cheek, thinking. "But this dress requires an upswept hairdo. Let's go a little more elaborate than your everyday style and have a few tendrils fall along the sides of your face."

Mary Ellen surprised herself by beginning to feel attractive enough to go out with Hawaii's most gorgeous man.

"Wonderful," Matilda said when they finished. "Now you're perfect for going out and. . .um. . .talking business." She laughed. "Ah! Keep that blush on your cheeks, and you're absolutely beautiful."

Mary Ellen felt a moment of doubt. "You think we've overdone it?"

fifteen

The moment Mary Ellen stood at the top of the stairs and saw him sitting in the living room with Rose, she knew outshining Mr. C. was impossible. He looked up and stood while she held on to the railing and descended the stairs.

Although he wasn't wearing a tuxedo with long tails, his suit seemed similar in style, and he wore a bowtie. His eyes were enhanced by the dark blue fabric as his glance swept over her.

A couple of times before, he had implied she was pretty. She'd thought he was making fun of her. But tonight, for the first time in her life, she felt beautiful. Would he tell her so?

Would she thank him without stammering?

She reached the bottom of the stairs, still holding on to the railing.

His gaze lingered for a moment before it moved to Matilda and Rose. "Now there's a dress fit for the queen."

"Yes," Matilda said. "But we don't have royalty anymore."

Mary Ellen's prepared *thank-you* was lost somewhere in her throat. He hadn't complimented her. And the stupid, stupid remark she heard herself say was, "Oh, but there's a sugar king."

Mortified, she had to swallow hard lest she choke. Matilda and Rose looked amused. Mr. C. plopped his top hat on his head. "Good evening, ladies," he said and escorted her out.

At the white car, he held open the door. With a sweep of his hand, he said, "Your royal coach, mademoiselle."

She hoped her response sounded like *merci*, and not *mercy*!

To her surprise, he did not head down the street to the Hilo Hotel. Instead, he drove in the opposite direction, along a strip of road above the beach, going higher into the hills.

The evening sun shone golden on the caps of the ocean waves. The palm branches swayed gently as the car passed. The fragrance of flowers filled the air. Mr. C. pointed out various plants and flowers and places as they drove by. He passed several horses and carriages along the way. Then a magnificent mansion rose on an incline. He parked where a sole black car sat.

"The grounds cover five acres," he said. "Would you like to stroll through some of the gardens before we go in?"

"Yes, I'd love it. This is so beautiful."

They walked along the paths in the gardens, exchanging greetings with other guests. He described the native plants, the palms, fruit trees, ferns, and orchids.

The hotel entrance looked like some wealthy person's parlor or living room. A man in a tuxedo was playing classical music on a grand piano. Several couples sat on couches, listening or talking.

Mr. C. walked Mary Ellen around the room, showing her pictures of royalty. "This is Queen Liliuokalani, who considered this one of her favorite places to dine.

"This might interest you. Do you know the author, Jack London?"

"Oh yes. He's a famous American writer. He was born in San Francisco." On a sadder note she added, "He wrote a lot of articles for *Collier's Magazine* about the earthquake and fire."

"I didn't know that." He smiled. "But I do know he stayed here for a month about three years ago."

The pianist and Clay nodded at each other as if they were acquainted. When they approached the entry into the dining room, a maître d' said, "Good evening, Mr. Honeycutt. Ma'am. Your usual table, sir?"

"Please," Mr. C. said. They were led through the dining room to a table in front of a wide window overlooking the bay below.

The waiter brought menus. After one glance, Mary Ellen had to say, "Much of this is Greek to me."

"Only the names," he said. "Mostly Hawaiian. A cow is a cow no matter how you pronounce it. But you might be interested in the *humuumunukunukuapuaa*."

"You're making that up."

He turned the menu and pointed. "Right here. And here's how it's pronounced: *whomoo-whomoo-newkoo-newkoo-ah-pu-ah-ah*. It's a fish. Repeat after me."

She did. And was about to laugh until she realized his focus was on her puckered lips. Well, if there was anything to Matilda's saying her blush made her look beautiful, she would look beautiful all evening.

She lowered the menu. "I've sampled a lot of fish already. I might like a steak. What would you suggest?"

"That's what I was thinking. Besides, we have to keep Mak in business. He has beef cattle and horse ranches."

"I'll take cattle, thank you."

He laughed lightly. "All right. Let's look at the steak entrées."

She read silently while he read aloud two of his choices. " 'Kalani's Kulana Big Island Kalbi Ribs with Nalo Farms Tatsoi Kimchi. Grass–fed, braised, boneless beef short ribs served with a sweet soy-ginger sauce, smoked sweet potato, Nalo Farms tatsoi and baby bok choy kimchi, and poblano-sweet pepper relish. Niman Ranch, Grilled, Roasted Garlic, Ribeye Steak with Hamakua Mushrooms. All natural, organic, grain-fed beef with a soy balsamic glaze, marinated ali'i oyster mushroom, wasabi-Dijon aioli, potatoes au gratin with smoked bacon, local tomatoes, and wild onions."

"The ribeye," she said.

"Great. I didn't know which I wanted. I'll have the kalbi ribs. We can taste each other's, if you wish."

She scoffed. "In a place like this?"

He shrugged. "Guests shouldn't be looking at anyone other than the persons at their own table."

She was glad he had said that. She hadn't really looked at anyone, or anything, but him.

The waiter must have been looking. As soon as Mr. C. laid the menus aside, the waiter came. Mr. C. ordered, and soon their fruity pineapple drinks were brought in long-stemmed glasses. He lifted his glass toward her, and she let her glass touch his. *"Mahalo nui loa,"* he said. "Thank you very much. To God, and to you."

She repeated, "Mahalo nui loa," assuming that was his blessing for the food to come. Silently, she was thanking God and Mr. C., too, for an evening in paradise as Cinderella. She would try to push aside the thought that midnight would come. The sun was turning a deeper gold. She'd seen enough of the Hawaiian sunsets to know that soon the depth and brilliance of color would be almost too beautiful to bear.

"Speaking of God," she said, facing him again, "Akemi's talking about God so freely has made me wonder if I've tried to play God with Breanna and Geoffrey. Who am I to say who should marry and when? Or what is God's will for another?"

"You're her sister. And you've tried to be like a mother to her."

"Yes. But I'm not her mother. And she's making her decisions apart from me. Maybe I'm just reluctant to let her go."

The waiter brought their food. It looked wonderful. She stared at it.

He said, "Would you like to say a blessing?"

She nodded. "Dear Lord, thank You for Your abundant blessings. Guide me, us as we discuss Breanna and Geoffrey. Help us to make decisions according to Your will. Amen."

He said, "Amen."

After a silence of cutting the meat and tasting, they agreed the food was delicious.

"I was afraid," Mary Ellen said after swallowing a few bites, "that Breanna was caught up in the idea of love. That's about all she and Akemi talk about. I suppose you know Akemi loves Jacob."

He nodded. "And he loves her."

"Then there was the beautiful weddings of the picture brides. There's the great romance of Jane and Mak I hear so much about. I see couples with eyes only for each other."

"Makes one feel rather left out, doesn't it?"

She glanced at him quickly. Had he reverted to his initial belief that she was after him? "I was speaking of Breanna. We've already picked out her wedding dress."

He waved his fork at her. She waited until he finished with the bite of food in his mouth.

"Keep sewing on those little pearls. I may know someone who would be perfect in that dress. It has to be the right person, because you've put your heart into it."

She nodded. Was Mr. C. getting wedding fever, too?

"And I've been thinking. If God sent Breanna here to find love, then He sent me to help her. Not hinder her." She didn't say so, but she wondered if she looked to others like a jealous spinster older sister. "I need to think of what she wants. I don't want to be their judge, to hold over them the threat of Geoffrey's imprisonment."

"What do you want?"

"I want her. . .to have a good life."

"Mary Ellen, what do you want for you?"

Mary Ellen? He called her by name without putting the *Miss* at the beginning or the *Colson* at the end. What did that mean?

It meant. . .that was her name.

Her fork played with the food on her plate. She remembered holding the wedding dress up and looking into the mirror. She had imagined Breanna in the dress with Mr. C. beside her. But the face in the mirror had been her own. Then came the reality of Matilda standing there.

❧

"Even little girls have dreams, don't they? I mean, even the picture brides value the wedding day although the next day, and every day for most of their lives, they will work in the fields."

"I'm not a little girl or a picture bride."

"No, but a man would be fortunate to have you as a bride. You're special, Mary Ellen. Has no one ever told you that?"

"Sure. Uncle Harv."

He stared. Until she had to laugh. Then he did.

"Then, you've never been kissed?"

She laughed lightly. "Well, I had a beau once. William."

"Oh. I am jealous."

She appreciated his trying to joke, to keep away any tension. The evening had been too good to allow that intrusion. She was more at ease with him than she had thought. Telling him about William came easily. But there wasn't much to tell, other than that they walked and rode together and shared a few kisses. "I knew I was too young to be serious. And I had Breanna to think of."

"Consider yourself told," he said in a serious tone, "by a man old enough to be your beau, and not your uncle or your young William, that you're special."

❧

Clay knew the color that rose to Mary Ellen's cheeks was not a reflection of the sunset. The guarded look he'd grown to recognize invaded her eyes. "Well, I am a blond." She looked mortified. "I should have said thank you."

"No you shouldn't. My reputation has preceded me, along with Geoffrey's actions. And, too, you came to Hawaii because of me."

She gazed at him so long he thought he might become lost in her eyes. The sky had turned red, but her eyes were soft and as light blue as a noontime sky. "Well," she said finally, "only indirectly. I'm here because of Geoffrey. Which reminds me. You called this meeting to talk about him, and I've done most of the talking."

Was that all their evening together meant to her? Or did she say that because he had intimated it was only to talk about Geoffrey?

"What I have to say about him is much like what you said about Breanna. He's not perfect, but basically good. He has some growing up to do, which I can say for a lot of us. But primarily, I wanted to talk about me. I didn't think you'd agree to this if I told you that earlier."

Those long lashes almost touched her cheeks as she lowered her eyelids. He felt she was not receptive to that. He was accustomed to women trying to impress him and asking all about the plantations, Hawaii, the sugar business and. . .him.

"To do that, however, I need to sweeten your attitude." He lifted his hand, and the waiter came. "Marlon, how about describing my favorite chocolate cake?"

"Yes, sir, Mr. Honeycutt. It is an unforgettable chocolate experience that combines layers of rich chocolate cake and semi-sweet chocolate ganache made with heavy cream and chocolate liqueur, all topped with slivers of milk chocolate."

"We'll have that."

"And Kona coffee," Marlon said, and Clay nodded.

He leaned toward her. "Almost daily, for all of my life, I've been surrounded by dark-haired, dark-eyed people. So it's refreshing to see a blue-eyed blond. I happen to like blond hair. But I don't hold it against a woman who isn't a blond. I'm not that small-minded."

"I wouldn't think that."

"But you may not think much of what I'm about to tell you. About me and Geoffrey."

"You don't have to tell me anything."

"Yes, I do. Because I'm the reason Geoffrey sent the photo to your office in San Francisco."

She didn't look surprised, just curious.

He was grateful Marlon chose that moment to bring the desserts.

He told her about the game. It had started innocently with him and Jacob meeting single women who came to the island. After Jacob decided that wasn't for him, Geoffrey had been eager to step in. "I'm not sure how it became like a contest, or game, to see who would escort the most blonds around the island. I was winning."

He felt like a loser. Her interest was focused on the cake instead of him.

"Like Geoffrey told you, that led to his sending my photo to the mainland. I don't think it was wrong to meet single women and take them out. But to make a game of it, turn it into some kind of contest, was wrong and disrespectful. Geoffrey is old enough to make his choices regardless of me. But I was the older, more mature one."

She had dug into that cake. At least she liked something. "You have a little bit of chocolate, right there." He almost reached over to touch the corner of her mouth, but quickly touched his own instead. What was he thinking? He wasn't.

"Thank you." She wiped the corner of her mouth with her napkin. After a sip of Kona, she looked directly at him. "I'm beginning to think age doesn't always make one more mature than another."

He nodded. "Geoffrey was wrong. But if anyone is to be punished, it should be me."

She seemed to study his eyes. Was she trying to see his soul? What kind of punishment would she want to enact? For Geoffrey, the punishment was she wouldn't let him get married. . .yet.

"I'm not doing that anymore," he said. "It's time I—" He stopped and looked down at his plate. If he was going to act maturely, this might be a good time to start. "Time I ate my cake."

He saw the sky turn gray, the ocean deep blue. But the lights in the dining room made the trim on her dress dance and gleam and sparkle. She was beautiful. And he had just confessed he wasn't going to do certain things anymore. Was that mature or foolish? Or a lie?

On the way back, she said, "Mahalo."

He looked over at her, and she explained. "For a wonderful evening. I've never had one like this. And thank you for confiding in me. I do appreciate it. How long would it take to wire San Francisco?"

Was she going back? Did she have someone to see there? William? "Two days at the most."

"I want to wire Uncle Harv so he can be here for Breanna's wedding."

At the house, he walked her to the door. Her glances made him think she was wondering what he might do. He wondered what she might do if he did.

"Mary Ellen."

She turned to look up at him. Little glass beads winked and twinkled at him. He folded his hands behind his back and held them there. "I want to invite you and Breanna to my place Friday night. She and Geoffrey can talk about their plans."

She nodded. Then she stared at him like he was out of his mind when he said, "I want to show you how I treat women I take to my plantation."

sixteen

Mary Ellen finally gave in to Breanna's pleading, and they bought the latest style in swimwear. Not the kind with stockings and skirts, but the one-piece with the legs halfway up the thighs. She definitely would not wear hers.

"I'm not sure we should go," Mary Ellen said to Matilda.

Matilda disagreed. "This is the perfect time for you to observe Geoffrey and Breanna and see if you think they're ready for marriage. Go. And have a good time."

Mary Ellen and Breanna wore comfortable, colorful *kohalas*. Clay and Geoffrey showed up in the car. They wore casual pants and flowered, short-sleeved shirts.

Mr. C. seemed so happy and carefree that Mary Ellen wondered if his confession of his wrongdoing had given him a clear conscience about the entire situation. Just what was he going to show her at his plantation?

They stopped at Mak's ranch, and she met him and the lovely Jane she'd heard so much about. Geoffrey wanted to show Breanna where he often trained horses that were used on Clay's plantation.

After leaving there, the car traveled along the dirt road across fenced pastureland where cows and horses grazed. Soon, Mary Ellen felt as if her heart were in her throat. Ahead were the fields Uncle Harv had talked about. Sugar-cane leaves as far as the eye could see, swaying gently in the breeze. She'd seen them in her day, and night, dreams.

The road ran through the fields. On each side were hundreds, perhaps thousands of men and women working, their heads covered with wide-brimmed hats. They were chopping, weeding, and cutting.

Clay and Geoffrey told the girls about the sugar-making

process and that one acre produced an average crop of three tons. Clay drove through the Japanese village, where a couple of women watched young children play.

"All this sugar supplies the world," Geoffrey said.

"And harvest is almost here," Clay added. "All this cane will be burned so it can be harvested."

He drove out of the fields and up and around an incline until they came to a lovely plantation home. They got out of the car. "This is where I live," Clay said.

"It's beautiful."

"Clay has a Japanese gardener. Can I show Breanna the gardens?"

"Sure," Clay said, and the young couple, hand in hand, scurried around the corner of the house.

"My parents built this," Clay said as he and Mary Ellen walked up onto the wide porch. He opened the door. "They enjoyed many years in it. I feel their absence here." She felt a stab of pain for him. Then he smiled. "Also I feel their presence."

She nodded. "Breanna and I felt the absence. And the shock." She took a deep breath. "Nothing was saved."

She liked the lanai best. She stood at the screen and looked out at the tropical flowers, trees, and ocean beyond.

"This is my favorite place," he said.

This setting could provide memories. Two people standing side by side in a favorite place, looking at the scenery. What was he thinking? She thought he began to turn toward her. But no. That was Breanna and Geoffrey coming around the house.

They got back into the car, and Clay drove them onto a narrow dirt lane, hardly wide enough for the vehicle to pass. Heavy foliage provided a canopy, and the late afternoon sun made lace of the shadows.

They emerged into the sunlight and drove between a row of palms and parked at the side of a small house. "My brother, Thomas, lived here," Clay said, "until after our parents died.

After he took over the business in Oahu, Geoffrey has stayed here. It's a relaxing, informal setting. The beach is private."

"Let's get into our bathing suits," Geoffrey said.

Mary Ellen was about to say she wasn't going to change, but as they walked around to the front she heard laughing and talking. People were getting out of a long canoe.

Her instinct was to say she thought the beach was private. But they all began to call to each other. Two females and three males were wearing much more revealing bathing suits than she and Breanna had brought. The males wore no shirts, but she'd become accustomed to that. Even in town, the men's shirts were often unbuttoned. That began to seem natural, like the men in canoes who greeted passenger ships.

In the middle of the floor, Mr. C. shucked out of his pants and shirt. Well yes, he certainly did look natural with most of his bronzed body showing, with its strong, rippling muscles, wide chest, broad shoulders, and trim waist. Geoffrey was equally well built, but something about Mr. C. made her feel. . . rather unnatural.

"I'll go on down," Clay said.

"Come on down when you're ready," Geoffrey said and ran outside.

Mary Ellen turned to Breanna, feeling her eyes were stuck open.

"I know," Breanna said. "Those are surfer bodies. But I've learned that's the natural look of Hawaii."

When they joined everyone else on the beach, Mary Ellen saw that Breanna was right. The three males had athletic builds. The females complimented each other's bathing suits, and from there nobody appeared to notice or care about bodies. They all had them.

They were all introduced, and Mary Ellen learned the strangers were friends, four of whom sang professionally and played ukuleles, along with their manager, the brother of one of the female singers. She couldn't pronounce some of their

Hawaiian names. The manager laughed. "Just say aloha, and we will answer."

Any thought of tension had vanished. Everything was fun and talk and getting to know each other. They made sandwiches together and ate at a wooden table beneath palms. They sat on the sand while the group sang, then taught Mary Ellen and Breanna some Hawaiian songs. Mary Ellen had only sung in church and was surprised how free and good she felt to sing aloud with this group. Clay and Geoffrey had wonderful voices.

While the sky turned orange, gold, crimson, pink, and scarlet, they set out on the vast sea in a canoe, seeming to be the only people in the world. They returned to shore, then screamed as they raced into the water to swim and play. Breanna explained to Mary Ellen, "Geoffrey taught me to swim better. And I tried surfing. All I do is fall." She laughed and swam out.

Mary Ellen walked along the edge of the shore, letting the water wash up on her feet and feel like it was pulling the sand out from beneath her feet. She had never felt so free, nor had so much fun.

"Come on in," Clay called.

"I'm not good in water. Don't bother with me. I'm fine."

She wasn't afraid, just not natural with it. The others, except Breanna were fish.

"I'll show you how," Clay said. "Here comes the wave. Now jump."

They played with the waves, pushed each other into the waves to see who could push the other under. She lost every time but liked the fun. They laughed and joked and pushed each other under.

Then she didn't see the others. Night had settled. She and Clay were farther out than she felt comfortable.

"You're okay. Come on."

They swam toward shore, and soon her feet could touch the bottom. She pushed him under. When he came up, she pushed at him. "That's for taking me out too far."

"It's not far. I can swim to that horizon."

"I don't see a horizon."

"That's my point."

His face seemed to be right at hers. His hands were on her shoulders. When a wave rocked them, his arms wrapped around her. He was shining, silver in the moonlight.

The waves pushed her closer. Something inside asked, *Must I go forever without really being kissed, except by a young boy? I'm in the arms of the most handsome man in Hawaii.* And he was looking at her like she was the only person. . .in the world.

She let the waves sway her. Or was it something inside herself, the man, the moon, the swaying palms, the songs, gentle nature, aloha love?

He was searing her soul, his eyes seeing. She closed them, raised her face to his, felt the warmth of his breath on her face, his intake of breath seemed to draw her own into his. She was losing herself.

His arms tightened, drew her even closer, and she could not stand were it not for his strong hands, her body against his, longing, yearning, then she felt his lips touch hers, no thought, or time, or place except his lips on hers, she was in the arms of her beloved, her love.

But her lips were longing for what did not come. The side of her face was against his bare chest and his hand was pressing her wet hair against her head. She felt two hearts beating as one, or was it only one, only hers? Strong arms wouldn't let her go. Suddenly, he let her go as a giant wave washed over them. Just as swiftly, he rescued her as he had been doing before they had stood so close together. He grabbed her hand and ran, almost pulling her onto the beach.

Others, that she had forgotten, laughed. He laughed. She had to laugh. She did not reach for a towel to wipe her face. It might get wet again from the ocean inside threatening her eyes.

Then she remembered he'd wanted to show her how he treated women. She'd been warned, but she'd played along anyway. His game. Lure a woman, charm her, prove she could not resist him.

She wasn't sure why she felt anger. Was it because he stopped the game before she experienced more than the brush of his lips across hers?

The friends began packing up their instruments and soon said their good-byes. Mary Ellen hurried into the house to change. She came out dressed in her casual clothes, with her hair towel dried.

Clay had slipped into his clothes. "Let's walk down the beach," he said.

"You. . .you're staring at me," she said.

He stopped, and so did she.

He reached out and touched her hair. Gently wound a strand around his finger. "Your hair looks silver in the moon-light." He paused. "I want to ask you something. I'd like to talk with you, Mary Ellen. Just the two of us. At my house. Geoffrey can take Breanna back. I have horses, carriages."

The sand felt like it did at the edge of the water, like it was being pulled out from under her. Was that the forerunner to asking her to spend the night? When they'd had dinner at the hotel, he'd been specific about saying he never coerced a woman.

It would be her decision.

What would she say?

She would be lost in his kiss. She'd already been lost in his arms.

Was that the kind of memory she wanted for the rest of her life?

Mary Ellen had not known she could be tempted to compromise her morals. But how did one know if she was really moral if she had never been tempted?

Yes, God must be in this, because although the thought occurred that a night with Claybourne Honeycutt would be wonderful, something inside warned that there was a tomorrow.

So far, all she'd lost was her voice.

When she said nothing, Clay gathered everyone in his car and drove past his house and through the fields of sugarcane, their leaves mocking beneath the silver moon, sounding like rain. Breanna and Geoffrey chatted happily and sang.

Once in a while, Breanna or Geoffrey asked her or Clay a question, and one responded. But they didn't say anything to each other.

After they returned to Hilo, Clay took her hand and led her to the side of the yard. "Mary Ellen, you have Breanna's wedding to plan, and I have a harvest to bring in. Will you think about giving me a chance to show you that I care about you and want to spend time with you? Will you think about it?"

Mary Ellen nodded. How could she ever not think about it?

❧

In the following days, time was taken up with planning Breanna's wedding, which would take place the day after Uncle Harv arrived. Matilda and Rose took Mary Ellen and Breanna to the house where they'd held the beach party to make sure some of the Japanese women could have it cleaned and ready for the married couple when they returned from their honeymoon.

Mary Ellen stood on the beach and looked at the ocean.

She thought about Clay's question.

On the day Uncle Harv was to arrive, Mary Ellen, Breanna, and Matilda stood on the dock. Uncle Harv was one of the first passengers to disembark, looking sprightly in his suit, top hat, and cane.

He seemed glad to see them all and hugged her first. Then Breanna. And Matilda after she put the lei over his head.

One of his first questions was to Breanna. "What's this about you getting married?"

She promised to tell him how it came about. Mary Ellen wasn't too sure how he'd take that. But for the present, he was pleased when Breanna said, "I want you to give me away."

Mary Ellen was about to climb into the backseat of Matilda's car beside Breanna when she saw Clay's car parked on the side street. She looked back and saw him and a beautiful brunette hurrying toward each other.

He swung her around. They hugged like they didn't want to let go. And kissed. It was brief, like a gentleman might kiss a lady in public. Their faces were close together as his arm went around her waist, and they walked toward his car. They were happy. . .with each other.

Mary Ellen jumped into the car and shut the door. The brunette obviously was no stranger to him. He was supposed to be busy at the plantation, getting ready for the harvest.

But he was with a beautiful brunette dressed in Western clothes.

He must think her very foolish. Had he deliberately manipulated her so she wouldn't go to the authorities about Geoffrey, which would involve his name? She was just another Western woman who fell under the spell of Claybourne Honeycutt. Even before she met him.

She threw herself into the wedding plans. There was much to do, although the wedding was to be small and casual.

Uncle Harv became open and fun-loving, even laughed about the photo incident and seemed to enjoy Breanna's love story. He took a room at the inn but came to the house often. After hours at the shop, Pilar began to show up to help with the wedding. The wedding day came. As maid of honor, Mary Ellen kept smiling, determined she was not going to spoil this day for her sister. And the blue tea gown Breanna had selected for her was lovely.

Geoffrey and Clay wore blue suits with light blue shirts, open at the neck as Breanna had requested. She didn't want the outdoor, daytime wedding to be too formal. The musicians who had been at the beach party all those days ago played Hawaiian music while Mary Ellen stood at one end of the arbor. . .and Clay on the other, not ten feet away. The pastor wore a white robe.

Uncle Harv walked Breanna down the aisle between the few chairs. Only a small group of people had been invited. Geoffrey's parents came from Oahu, along with Clay's sister and brother with their families. They were joined by the pastor's wife, Akemi, and a few of Matilda's special friends from church.

Mr. Hammeur and his wife were delighted to have been invited. Pilar came. Breanna looked perfect in the dress she'd chosen. A couple of Geoffrey's and Clay's friends came. And a photographer.

Uncle Harv had paid for the bridal suite on the cruise ship they would take around the islands on their honeymoon. Clay drove the bride and groom down in his car.

Breanna and Geoffrey would change clothes at Matilda's before leaving for the dock. There would not be a reception, but there would be a cake and fruit drinks for the couple, along with Mary Ellen, Uncle Harv, Pilar, Matilda, Rose, Akemi, Clay, the pastor, and his wife.

They piled in their cars and carriages and drove past the dock and along the main street of Hilo to Matilda and Rose's house.

Mary Ellen didn't want to think it, but she couldn't help it. Where was Clay's brunette? She hadn't been invited to the wedding, so she might be at his house. Perhaps he didn't play games with brunettes, just took them seriously.

"Yes, the cake is delicious. Matilda made it."

"Wonderful punch. Have some more."

Clay would probably drive Breanna and Geoffrey to the dock. She would be expected to accompany her sister. But rather than having to make excuses, as soon as Breanna had changed, Mary Ellen said, "I'm going to say my good-byes right here, instead of at the dock."

They hugged.

Soon after the bridal couple left, the guests did, as well.

Matilda said, "This has been trying on you. Rose and I will

clean up in here. You take it easy."

Mary Ellen nodded. "I'd like to walk out back for a while."

She walked across the yard, through the trees, and farther than she'd meant. Before long, she could see the beach and the ocean. What would she do now? What should she do? She had no reason to stay in Hawaii. She could use her sister as an excuse. But her sister was now a married woman.

She had. . .Uncle Harv.

"Mary Ellen."

She jumped, not from fear but from recognizing the voice.

"What's wrong?" he said. "You've ignored me all day."

"There's nothing for us to talk about. I won't be just another blond in your game."

He stepped around to face her. "I thought you understood."

She turned away. "Oh yes, I understand."

He gave a short laugh. "I guess I was egotistical enough to think you cared about me, that our dinner at the hotel was special, and the night at the beach. It was for me. I'm sorry."

Special to him? Yes, enough for him to want to spend time with her. Maybe she would even call him back, but her throat hurt and her eyes stung.

He was already striding away.

seventeen

The next morning, Mary Ellen went down to the kitchen. Uncle Harv was there. Matilda and Rose were fixing breakfast. She said good morning as cheerfully as she could, but had one more action to take before she could turn her hourglass life right side up.

"Be right back." She walked out to the back porch and stood beside the trash can. She would look one last time before tearing it into little pieces.

"Could I see?" Matilda stepped out.

Why not?

"This is what started it all? The little flame in your heart?"

"Doesn't everyone say all the women fall for him?"

"True. But I've never known him to put forth the effort he has with you. If a woman isn't interested, he can simply have another."

"He has another. But that's his business. I saw him hug and kiss a woman."

"When was that?"

"When we picked up Uncle Harv."

"A brunette about your age?"

Mary Ellen nodded.

"Oh, honey. That's Leia. Jane and Mak's daughter. There're like sister and brother. He met her to take her to the ranch. She had only one day here before going to Oahu for an equestrian show. She's been on the mainland for several months. Rose said Leia is serious about a man she met on the mainland. He's coming here in a few weeks."

Mary Ellen felt her shoulders slump, and she returned the photo to her pocket.

"Come inside, Mary Ellen."

She gasped. "Uncle Harv. You heard?"

"You're my niece. I have a right to hear."

She hurried inside, and they hugged. Her puffy eyes probably hung to her chin by now.

"I want to tell you a story," he said. "Drink your coffee and listen."

She did, and he began.

"Mary Ellen, back in San Francisco, I believed you wanted the Hawaiian adventure but was afraid to take it. After I arrived here and Breanna told me about that photo, everyone laughed or smiled except you. You've always put what she wanted first."

"What kind of sister would I be if I hadn't?"

"Not nearly the sweet, wonderful girl you are. But sometimes, fear keeps us from reaching out. I've never told anyone this in my life."

Glancing around, he smiled tentatively but didn't ask Matilda and Rose to leave. They settled back against their chairs.

"I came to Hawaii on one of the first steamship voyages. On that trip, I met a lovely widow a few years older than I, and we were inseparable. My business was here, and she went on to Maui to see a brother. I didn't accept her invitation to visit, using work as an excuse."

Mary Ellen could feel his sadness as he continued. "After she returned to England, she invited me to visit. For a long time, I did not write. But I was miserable and finally admitted that I loved her and wanted to have a life with her."

He shook his head. "But by the time she received my letter, it was too late. She had married a good man and was in the family way. Since then, I've tried to stifle my emotions." He glanced around and smiled. "But the last time I came to Hawaii, Matilda and Rose cracked my shell. Now, I've been introduced to a widow and am trying not to fear what may or may not happen."

She thought he was talking about Pilar.

"I was afraid to love you and Breanna. Love requires so much of a person. And with it comes the chance of being hurt."

"Uncle Harv, I love you." She went to him, and he held her tight.

Then he let go. "Stop this, young lady. You're smearing my glasses, and I can't see a thing."

She moved away, smiling at him.

Then he admonished, "If you're going to err, Mary Ellen, err on the side of love."

&

That morning, she went to the church to pray and think. As if the Lord Himself had spoken, Mary Ellen knew she had to do it. She needed to ask Clay's forgiveness for her attitude toward him. She'd been rude and judgmental. And Uncle Harv had made her see she had been afraid. Not of Mr. C. so much, but of her own feelings.

She hadn't wanted to be hurt.

But she was hurting.

"I need to see him," she said upon returning to the house. Rose said she and Matilda wanted Uncle Harv to meet Mak and Jane. They could all go to the ranch, then someone would take her to the plantation.

After they reached the ranch, Mak chose a horse for her. "But I'll go with you. I need to talk with Clay."

She was grateful for his company. Without him, she might have felt fear since she hadn't ridden in a long time and never over such a long stretch of road.

Mak stopped at the mill near a field, and they dismounted. Mary Ellen was trying to converse with a woman walking with little children. They had to make a lot of hand motions and smile and nod to make themselves clear. The children began copying them, and they all laughed.

When Mak came out, he said Clay was at a field a couple of miles away where they were burning the cane. "You stay here at the mill. I'll get him."

"Maybe I should wait until he's not busy."

"He can usually get away if he needs to."

He rode away.

Mary Ellen began to doubt. Suppose he thought her apology trivial. She walked toward the miles of sugarcane, its leaves swaying like waves on the ocean.

A fanciful dream crossed her mind. Why not let the dream of walking in the sugarcane become a reality? If Mr. C. rode down, she could call to him and watch him stride toward her. That will be a memory to have with her forever.

She felt a tug on her arm and turned. The woman was saying no, no, and shaking her head. The children stood back at the mill, watching.

"It's okay. I won't go far." She stepped inside the cane that came to her shoulders. She looked back when the woman began yelling and running toward the children. One of them must have done something wrong.

The cane became thicker. She was getting into stalks higher than her head. But all she'd have to do was go back through the row. When she turned, the cane was still higher than her head, and rows led in every direction. Which would take her out? How far had she come?

She smelled smoke. Turning, she saw that it was all around her. It wasn't just smoke. She could feel the heat, smell the sugar, see the flames, hear the crackling of the cane as it burned.

She could scream, but who could hear above the rush of flames overtaking the fields? Her throat felt dry and tight.

The air was thick and smoky. She felt. . .faint.

She thought someone called her name. That was probably her imagination. She'd heard that when people died they saw a light. She was seeing fire, and darkness. Yes, she heard her name.

"Here. I'm here."

"Mary Ellen." She heard horse's hooves, but it was too dark to see. She could barely make out a horse and rider.

She kept coughing out. "I'm here! I'm here!"

A horse and rider passed, and she screamed. It turned and came back. She was snatched up and thrown onto the horse. They were headed straight into high flames. Her skirt was jerked up over her head and an arm held her close to his chest. She could hardly breathe.

"Hold tight."

She felt the fire as they went through it. Then she was being unwrapped and water was thrown on her. She coughed and wheezed but managed to get a few gulps of breath down her raw throat. She was sitting on the ground. The woman who'd tried to keep her from the cane put something on her burned leg.

She was given something to drink. Then she saw Clay stretched out on the sand. What were they doing? Was he all right? Mak was smearing something on Clay's face and on his arms.

Japanese and Caucasians stared at her. They knew this was her fault. Mak glanced at her. "Aloe," he said. "It will help the burn."

"I'm all right," Clay mumbled.

"He will be," Mak said. "He was just scared out of his wits. He knew the men were on the horses, ready to burn this field. Fortunately, the woman ran into the mill and they wired the next mill. But not in time to stop the fires from being set."

Clay tried to sit. He took the liquid offered him. Mary Ellen didn't know what it was, but it made her throat feel better.

Clay rasped. "I've never prayed so hard." He coughed.

"Let's get more of this on your face and arms," Mak said. "Then we have to get you to the hospital."

"Hospital," he croaked out. "Why?"

Why?

No one said it, but it was because the man who had women fall at his feet over his looks had a face as red as a crimson sunset.

Asking his forgiveness for her attitude seemed minor now. Mary Ellen was responsible for destroying the face of the best-looking man in Hawaii.

eighteen

They wanted to keep Clay overnight at the hospital. After everybody visited him, the one he really wanted to see appeared in the doorway. She knocked softly but didn't enter until he asked her to come in.

"The doctor said you'll be fine," he said.

She nodded. "The place on my leg is like a bad sunburn. Thank you for protecting the rest of me."

"I should have been more clear when I talked about harvest and burning the cane. I take for granted everyone knows the fires can be set at any time and they burn quickly."

"I thought the cane would be cut before it was burned. It never occurred to me the fields would be set on fire."

"Why did you go in there?"

She sat in the chair and told him the most fantastic story about the photo and about her dreams of him running toward her in the sugarcane fields.

She called that foolish.

"I've been a problem to Breanna and Geoffrey since I came here. And now look what I've done to you."

His throat was raw, and he wasn't supposed to talk, but he had to, if she would listen.

"For quite a while now, it's as if God was whispering to me, and then you came shouting at me."

As best she could, through her raspy throat, she said, "I didn't shout at you."

"Same as. You asked about the significance of things, like that church steeple being one hundred feet high."

She shrugged. "I was just curious."

"Right. But I kept thinking about it. I asked Jacob, and he told me to figure it out. In reading about the history of the church, something jumped out at me. The church is one hundred feet long. Before Jacob left for the mainland, I asked him again. He said he didn't know and hoped I'd tell him."

Clay started to laugh, but that hurt his throat. He was talking too much. He drank some water.

"Maybe you shouldn't talk."

"I know. But I need to. I want you to know." He waited for the water to soothe his throat. "I thought of the steeple being one hundred feet high, reaching toward God. The church is one hundred feet long. Reaching across the earth. One's reach on earth should not exceed one's reach for God. I have a lot of sugarcane on this red earth of Hawaii. What I have with God has fallen far short of that."

"You've mentioned God a lot, like you know Him."

"Oh, I do. I'm part of this group descended from the early missionaries. I know we each have to make the decision to follow Christ, but there is a faith that seems inbred in us. It's a part of us that we can't deny."

He told her about his giving his heart to Jesus when he was nine years old. "And no matter how much I've tried to ignore it, deep inside, it's like the little boy in me is on the rope in the steeple, ringing the bell, saying, look up, farther than the sugarcane fields."

Clay watched her look down. But she had spoken her heart. He wanted to do that. "It's as if God said '*Reach for Me.*' I did, and you know what? His hand was no farther than mine. I was already in His arms the moment my thoughts, my commitment went to Him. Maybe that's why He allowed me to become burned and ugly. What I had to attract anyone is gone."

She looked up quickly. "At this moment, there could be no man more appealing than you."

If his throat would let him, he'd scoff at that. "I don't know if I'll ever look the same. The skin may clear. It may be scarred. But it will take time before it's healed."

Mary Ellen spoke softly. "You've never looked better to

me. You were my knight in shining armor, on a white horse, coming to rescue me."

"My horse is black."

"It's the perception that matters. You rescued me." She hesitated. "But I thought horses were afraid of fire."

"Mine are trained to run through fire and to jump over it. When fires are set, there's the possibility of someone being caught between fields. Things can go wrong."

"Well, I'm grateful. I'm sorry about your face. But what I see of you now is the inside. I respect and admire that. I know you're a good person. And any decent woman would not love someone just because they're good looking."

"Did you say *love*?" He reached and caught her hand.

"No. I said I could *not* love."

She tried to pull away, but he would not allow it. "Could you love someone who has been foolish, played a dangerous game, and hurt you in the process? Could you forgive a person like that?"

"I suppose I've been foolish in my lifetime."

"Really? When?"

"I've tried to run Breanna's life. I've judged you. I saw a photo and imagined impossible dreams. I also accused you of being a villain. Can you forgive me?"

"For thinking of me as a villain, yes. Although I'm afraid I have been. Not in a criminal way, but in toying with women's hearts, although that was not my intent. My pride and ego needed that to make me feel worthwhile. I know now that doesn't do it."

"What does?"

"What I've been taught. The Lord Jesus in our hearts and lives. I knew that. But I got away from it. And. . .I heard you praying for me out there in the hall when you wouldn't come in here. I am eternally grateful. If forgiveness is due, I offer mine."

"I forgive you, too. You found Breanna for me. Because of your photo, my sister is in love with Geoffrey and these islands. I think they were meant for each other."

"Do you think I'm worthy to have a wonderful woman love me?"

"I know you are"

"Someone as wonderful and beautiful as you?"

"I'm not—"

"Yes, you are. Outside and in. I've had to ask myself, who and what am I? I want to start over. I know I can. In fact, I have by asking God's forgiveness for my not taking life and women more seriously."

"Don't feel too badly. If you had, then Breanna and Geoffrey might never have met."

"Nor. . .you and I?"

"Is that so important?"

"Next to learning how to live my life for the Lord, it's the most important thing to me. Could you, would you, consider giving me another chance? Like you did the day we met and gave me the chance to prove my innocence. . .which proved my guilt?"

"That's a little complex. I'd like to think about it."

Her hand left his. She stood. He watched her turn, and it felt like a knife turning in his heart.

Abruptly, she faced him again. "I thought about it. Yes, I'll give you a chance. If you give me one."

&

Mary Ellen was afraid to hope Clay was talking about her in that hospital room. Maybe he meant women in general. But now, they could relate. She would not have unrealistic dreams, but she could keep her memories and relate to Clay as her sister's husband's friend.

But she could also relate to Akemi's having said it would be hard to live in the world with him, and without him.

Several days passed, along with the talk about the fire and the close call she and Clay had. No one seemed to blame her for the trouble she'd caused.

A few days later, the postman delivered a letter for her to

the dress shop. Inside was a photo of Clay. On the back, was a note:

> Wanted: An American blond with blue eyes.
> If interested, come to the Matti-Rose Inn
> 7 o'clock Friday evening.
> Mr. C. Honeycutt

Mary Ellen wore the coral-colored holoku that she'd tried on in the dress shop the day Clay had seen her play-dancing.

Matilda led her into the dining room and to a table covered with a white tablecloth. On it was a beautiful floral centerpiece. Akemi brought two glasses with pineapple nectar in them.

After she was seated, Clay appeared in the doorway, dressed in a white suit and a colorful shirt, open at the neck. In his hand, he held a flowered lei. He came up to her and arranged it around her neck.

His face was splotchy and peeling, but that didn't matter. What mattered was the warmth in his deep blue eyes. She was seeing him with her heart, and he was beautiful.

"Thank you for coming," he said.

"Thank you for inviting me."

He held her hands. The man who had raced through smoke and fire to rescue her, now trembled in this safe, calm, beautiful setting.

She hoped she knew why.

He took a deep breath. "I never thought I would say this. But Mary Ellen Colson, I'm in love with you."

She closed her eyes. When she opened them, he was still there holding her hands.

She felt her body tremble. And her hands. And her lips.

"Will you marry me?"

She was nodding. Yes. Yes.

He took a little box from his pocket. Sitting on blue velvet was the ring she had admired when she and Matilda had looked at rings with Breanna.

He slipped it on her finger.

"I love it. It is so beautiful." Her smile trembled. "But what it means is the important thing."

"And it means I love you and want to spend the rest of my life with you."

"I want that, too. I love you." After a moment, she said, "How did you know the size?"

"Matilda said you had tried on a pair of gloves in the dress shop."

"So a lot of people were in on this."

He shrugged. "Maybe. . .only. . .the entire island."

"What made you think I would accept this?"

"You mean besides your eyes being the mirror of your soul? Your not being able to stay away from me although I often acted like a heel? Your keeping my old photo in your skirt pocket?"

"How—"

"People talk. And," he added, "Matilda told me that women ignore only men they're in love with. And one other thing. I prayed to God that He would make you love me. See, you didn't stand a chance."

"You'd better stop while you're ahead, Mr. C."

Akemi said, "Kiss your bride-to-be."

Mary Ellen saw him look at her lips; then he grinned. "No way. Not here."

She was grateful. He, too, must be remembering when they were swept away, like a wave disappearing over the ocean. Even though they had not kissed.

His eyebrows lifted. "We need to set a date for the wedding."

epilogue

Mary Ellen planned the traditional American part of the wedding. Clay added the Hawaiian touch. It seemed everyone else wanted to plan the reception. Finally, Clay settled it.

"Plan what you like. But not until we return from our honeymoon." He wouldn't tell her where they would be.

She couldn't have dreamed a more wonderful wedding. After the guests were seated, a Hawaiian love song was sung by Clay's friend who had been at the party. His sister, in a sleeveless, rose-colored dress and wearing a white lei moved her graceful arms and hands. Her body barely moved like a tide caressing the shore, or a palm frond swaying in a gentle breeze.

The beauty of it lingered, even as Clay and the pastor entered from a side door. Breanna and Geoffrey walked down the aisle together as matron of honor and best man.

Uncle Harv escorted Mary Ellen down the aisle toward the most handsome man in the world, dressed in a black tuxedo. His face had healed, but that's not what was so appealing. It was him, his heart, his soul, and she loved him. She would love him if he were not handsome.

Breanna and Geoffrey handed each of them a white lei, and they put them around the other's neck. Mary Ellen hardly knew what the pastor was saying but managed to repeat after him and say *I do* at the right time. She and Clay knelt while his friends sang "Amazing Grace."

They stood, and the pastor pronounced them man and wife. "You may kiss the bride."

Mary Ellen saw that challenge, that dare in Clay's eyes and felt the rest of the world fading. His face came near. She lifted hers, her lips begging for his touch. She could feel his warm breath on her lips. He barely grazed them, then whispered in her ear, "Not yet."

The pastor introduced them as Mr. and Mrs. Claybourne Honeycutt.

After being showered with flower petals, they began saying their good-byes. "Uncle Harv, don't leave here before I get back."

"Who knows?" he said. "I may quit my job and work with Mr. Hammeur. After all, Akemi says she's going to college." He and Pilar smiled at each other. . .in that special way.

Yes, Mary Ellen had to admit, Hawaii was a paradise for love and romance.

"For now," Clay said impatiently, "it's time we left on the yacht."

"Yacht?" Mary Ellen said. "What yacht?"

"Your yacht."

"I don't have a yacht."

"It's your wedding present."

"That's. . .I mean, yachts are expensive."

His eyebrows lifted, and his eyes challenged. "Haven't you heard? I'm the sugar king."

Later on the ship, she said, "I fell in love with you the moment I saw your photo. When did you know you were in love with me?"

"When I first saw you through the window of the dress shop, sewing little pearls on a wedding dress. I resented each time you said it would be worn by Breanna. I didn't know that I loved you then, but I know it now. And here you are."

He started to touch the pearls and moved his hand away.

"It's all right to touch them now," she said. "They're yours. Everything I am and have is yours."

He touched them. He touched her face and her lips. "Now, I am going to kiss you." His fingers on her lips were replaced by his lips, and beneath the golden moonlight and cool breeze, the sound of gentle waves caressing the yacht, they kissed, a deep, long, meaningful, belonging-to-each-other-under-God's-heaven kind of kiss. His fingers entwined in her long blond hair, hanging loose.

She leaned back only a little. "I feel like I belong to Hawaii and you, Mr. C."

"You do, Mrs. C.," he said meaningfully, looking at his bride. "You are so beautiful. Just like I've pictured you."

A Letter To Our Readers

Dear Reader:

In order that we might better contribute to your reading enjoyment, we would appreciate your taking a few minutes to respond to the following questions. We welcome your comments and read each form and letter we receive. When completed, please return to the following:

Fiction Editor
Heartsong Presents
PO Box 719
Uhrichsville, Ohio 44683

1. Did you enjoy reading *Picture Bride* by Yvonne Lehman?
   ❑ Very much! I would like to see more books by this author!
   ❑ Moderately. I would have enjoyed it more if

   _____

   _____

   _____

2. Are you a member of **Heartsong Presents**? ❑ Yes ❑ No
   If no, where did you purchase this book? _____

   _____

3. How would you rate, on a scale from 1 (poor) to 5 (superior), the cover design? _____

4. On a scale from 1 (poor) to 10 (superior), please rate the following elements.

   ____ Heroine   ____ Plot
   ____ Hero   ____ Inspirational theme
   ____ Setting   ____ Secondary characters

5. These characters were special because? _____

_____

_____

6. How has this book inspired your life? _____

_____

_____

7. What settings would you like to see covered in future
   Heartsong Presents books? _____

_____

_____

8. What are some inspirational themes you would like to see
   treated in future books? _____

_____

_____

9. Would you be interested in reading other **Heartsong
   Presents** titles? ❏ Yes ❏ No

10. Please check your age range:
    ❏ Under 18   ❏ 18-24
    ❏ 25-34   ❏ 35-45
    ❏ 46-55   ❏ Over 55

Name _____

Occupation _____

Address _____

City, State, Zip _____

HEARTSONG
P R E S E N T S

If you love Christian romance…

$10.⁹⁹

You'll love Heartsong Presents' inspiring and faith-filled romances by today's very best Christian authors…Wanda E. Brunstetter, Mary Connealy, Susan Page Davis, Cathy Marie Hake, and Joyce Livingston, to mention a few!

When you join Heartsong Presents, you'll enjoy four brand-new, mass-market, 176-page books—two contemporary and two historical—that will build you up in your faith when you discover God's role in every relationship you read about!

Mass Market 176 Pages

Imagine…four new romances every four weeks—with men and women like you who long to meet the one God has chosen as the love of their lives…all for the low price of $10.99 postpaid.

To join, simply visit www.heartsong presents.com or complete the coupon below and mail it to the address provided.

- -

YES! Sign me up for Heartsong!

NEW MEMBERSHIPS WILL BE SHIPPED IMMEDIATELY!
Send no money now. We'll bill you only $10.99 postpaid with your first shipment of four books. Or for faster action, call 1-740-922-7280.

NAME _____

ADDRESS_____

CITY_____ STATE ____ ZIP _____

MAIL TO: HEARTSONG PRESENTS, P.O. Box 721, Uhrichsville, Ohio 44683
or sign up at WWW.HEARTSONGPRESENTS.COM